ONLY
ONE FOOT
TO THE EAST

A tale of overcoming adversity,
travel adventure, acceptance,
and finding love

Matthew R James

DEDICATION

To the resilient spirits who have faced adversity and emerged stronger, to those who dared to challenge the status quo, and to the dreamers who never gave up on finding their own path. This story is dedicated to you – the rebels, the healers, the lovers, and the seekers of truth. It is a tribute to the strength of the human spirit, the power of forgiveness, and the unwavering belief in the possibility of a better tomorrow.

It is also dedicated to the memory of those lost to the darkness of addiction, a stark reminder of the fragility of life and the importance of compassion in a world that often forgets. For those who fought for a more just and equitable society during the turbulent 1970s, and for those who continue that fight today, this is a testament to your bravery and unwavering commitment to change.

May this story serve as a reminder that even amidst chaos and uncertainty, hope endures, and the journey of self-discovery is a lifelong pursuit, worthy of celebration and profound understanding. And finally, to all those who have ever held a secret, carried a burden, or found solace in unexpected places – may this tale resonate with your own unspoken experiences and help you find your way home.

CONTENTS

PREFACE 1

CHAPTER ONE *The Aftermath of the Crash* 3

CHAPTER TWO *Before the Crash – Part 1* 16

CHAPTER THREE *Brian – Early Life, Part One* 30

CHAPTER FOUR *Before the Crash – Part Two* 37

CHAPTER FIVE *Brian – Early Life, Part Two* 46

CHAPTER SIX *Before the Crash – Part Three* 54

CHAPTER SEVEN *Rehabilitation – a New Reality* 66

CHAPTER EIGHT *The Trip is Planned* 76

CHAPTER NINE *The Journey Begins – Europe* 82

CHAPTER TEN *The Journey Continues – Asia* 88

CHAPTER ELEVEN *India – Part One* 95

CHAPTER TWELVE *India – Part Two* 104

CHAPTER THIRTEEN *India – Part Three* 117

CHAPTER FOURTEEN *Australia – Part One* 138

CHAPTER FIFTEEN *Australia – Part Two* 148

CHAPTER SIXTEEN *Picking Up the Pieces* 154

CHAPTER SEVENTEEN *Lucy at University* 170

CHAPTER EIGHTEEN *Courtship* 180

AFTERWORD 187

ACKNOWLEDGEMENTS 195

APPENDIX 197

ABOUT THE AUTHOR 198

PREFACE

This story began as three separate strands that I wanted to explore: firstly, that of a young and beautiful woman who suddenly has to come to terms with the results of an accident that leaves her permanently disabled, an amputee, and how she adjusts, slowly building resilience and coming to acceptance, and a deeper and more fulfilling life; secondly, the phenomenon of attraction to amputees, in both positive and negative aspects; and thirdly, the social 'revolution' that was the hippy era – flower power, cannabis, psychedelic drugs, the anti-war movement, the search for spiritual enlightenment, the hippy trail to India – and the darker underbelly – drug smuggling, and addiction.

The vibrant, turbulent era of the nineteen-sixties and seventies is a time often romanticised, yet fraught with complexities – a period of societal upheaval, youthful rebellion, and a search for meaning in a world rapidly changing. I wanted to explore this period, not through rose-tinted glasses, but with a candid look at its shadows and its light. Lucy's journey, born from both the ashes of a motorbike accident and of her involvement in the counterculture of the time, reflects the metaphorical and literal journeys we all undertake in the pursuit of self-discovery. Her unconventional choices, her struggle with coming to terms with a life-changing accident, and her confrontation with the darker side of the counterculture, create a tapestry woven with threads of both hope and despair. I have endeavoured to portray Lucy's experiences with honesty and sensitivity, exploring themes of physical and emotional healing, the challenging of established views (religious, societal, and moral), the quest for deeper spiritual meanings, the consequences of our actions, and the unwavering power of human connection.

Through her story, and through those of her male companions, Zak and Brian, I hope to illuminate the resilience of the human spirit, the capacity for change, and the beauty of finding love and meaning amidst adversity. This book is not merely a tale of smuggling and escape, of adversity and love; it's a coming-of-age story that speaks to the universal quest for belonging, authenticity, and a future shaped by our own choices. I hope you will join Lucy on her journey, and that it will leave you pondering your own path towards self-discovery, reminding you of the importance of facing your past and embracing a brighter future, while knowing that only the present is real.

CHAPTER ONE

The Aftermath of the Crash

The smells of both antiseptic and burnt rubber still clung to Lucy's memory, a phantom scent that lingered even after months had passed since the crash. The image, too, remained stubbornly etched onto her mind's eye: the screech of tyres on asphalt, the sickening crunch of metal, the blinding flash of pain before a merciful oblivion swallowed her whole.

She had woken up in the bare clinical environment of a cubicle in the Accident and Emergency department in a hospital, the throbbing in her body and especially her leg and her abdomen a constant, dull ache that overshadowed the duller, more persistent ache in her heart. The doctors were blunt, efficient, their words a brutal surgical incision into her youthful idealism. Her crash helmet had probably saved her from being killed, but she had suffered multiple injuries, very serious ones to her leg, possibly equally serious ones to her abdomen, and a number of other less serious injuries. They would need to operate as soon as possible, to save her life, regardless of whether she or a relative was capable of giving consent. Lucy was unable to sign anything, and just wanted to be out of the excruciating pain she was in, so gave verbal consent. She was immediately given sedatives, and drifted back into unconsciousness.

She woke up a second time in intensive care, a tube up her nose, a drip in her left arm, her right arm immobilised. A nurse checked her pulse, noted that she was awake, and offered her a sip of water.

Her mouth was dry, her tongue seemed twice the normal size, and her throat burned, so the water came as an all-too-brief respite.

Once she was more fully awake the doctors came again. The leg, they'd said, they had been trying to save, but in all probability it would not be possible. The knee had been crushed into a pulp, the bones shattered and fragmented, and despite attempts to restore arteries and veins, there was only the slightest pulse in the lower leg, and the lower part of the thigh had been degloved – effectively stripped of skin and subcutaneous flesh, with a compound fracture of the femur (that is, with the bone protruding through the flesh). If infection could be controlled and the leg saved, and it was a big if, she would undergo months of traction, skin grafts and further operations, would always have a stiff and half-useless leg, would probably have to use crutches, and might even require a wheelchair. Amputation above the knee, through the upper thigh, was probably a better option.

Due to extensive bruising on her abdomen the doctors had also feared she might have internal abdominal injuries – pelvic fractures, a ruptured spleen or a torn bowel – and they had therefore both x-rayed her pelvis (which was, fortunately, intact) and performed a laparotomy, an incision from two inches above her navel for seven inches down the centre line of her abdomen. Their fears had been partly correct – she did indeed have a torn colon, and consequent peritonitis – an infection of the abdominal cavity caused by leakage of faecal matter from the torn intestine. As a result they had washed out her abdominal cavity, had removed part of her colon and had given her a colostomy, which they thought could probably be reversed at a later stage if she recovered satisfactorily from her other injuries. Therefore she now had a stoma (a round blob that looked like a large cherry, but was in fact the cut-off end of her colon brought out through an incision in the front of her abdomen) with a bag stuck over it onto her tummy, which collected her poo, and of course she was left with a scar down her tummy.

Lucy was devastated. She could not initially bring herself to accept the recommendation to amputate her leg, but within twenty-four hours a serious infection set in, which, with the limited circulation resulting from the crush injuries, could not be adequately controlled with intravenous antibiotics, and which threatened to re-infect her already traumatised abdomen, if not her entire body. Running a fever and drifting in and out of delirium, Lucy was left with no choice.

Within a few hours Lucy's left leg was amputated high above the knee, leaving her with less than a third of her thigh, and, unknown to her or to her doctors, a dormant infection – osteomyelitis – buried deep in the sawn-off stump of her femur.

As well as the injuries to her leg and abdomen Lucy had a number of other injuries – a broken right wrist, cracked ribs, cuts and bruises – but these paled into insignificance compared to the damage to and loss of her leg. She was initially in intensive care, hooked up to a nasogastric tube (a plastic tube taped to her cheek, which went up her nose and down into her stomach), a drip in her left arm providing blood, saline, and antibiotics (her broken right wrist was encased in a plaster cast), a drain in the incision where her leg had been amputated, and a catheter in her bladder, and – of course   her colostomy bag. Apart from the latter, after a few days most of this was disconnected, and she was moved onto a ward.

The initial shock had been devastating. Then anger, a raw, burning fury that threatened to consume her, was only slightly less intense than the physical pain. This anger was directed at the tractor driver for his carelessness (she learned later that the farmer driving the tractor was the one who had called the ambulance, effectively saving her life), at the doctors for not having saved her leg, and most of all at herself, for having been stoned when riding her motorbike and for going too fast round a blind bend. The physical pain threatened at times to overwhelm her. What was strange about it was that she could feel the pain all the way down into the foot of the leg she no longer had. The nurses explained to her that this was perfectly normal, that most amputees suffered to a greater or lesser extent with 'phantom limb pain', and that it was probable that this would subside over time – though Lucy might never be completely free of it. The pain in her abdomen was also intense, and at times it felt like her whole insides were being squeezed out through the new hole that was her stoma.

Lucy, a free spirit who'd spent her teenage years gradually embracing the boundless energy of the 1970s counterculture, like a butterfly emerging from its cocoon, suddenly found herself tethered to a world of limitations. The vibrant tapestry of her life, once rich with the colours of freedom and self-expression, was now frayed and torn, its threads hopelessly tangled. The bike, her beloved Honda 50, a symbol of her independence, was a crumpled wreck, a stark reflection of her own shattered body and spirit.

The biggest shock was when she was able to see herself in a mirror, and the empty space, where her leg should have been, hit her almost like a physical blow. By this time her mother had brought in her spare pair of glasses, replacing the ones broken in the crash. Being short-sighted, Lucy needed glasses to see anything clearly, so she was now able to see her own reflection.

Although the physical rehabilitation was good, at that time there was little or no psychological support or counselling for people who suffered life-changing injuries through accidental trauma. Lucy relied on her mother, and her boyfriend Zak (though she tried always to ensure that her mother and Zak saw her separately, as they didn't get on). But it was chiefly on her own inner strength and resources, which she hadn't even been aware that she had, that she relied most. She squarely faced the fact that her life had changed irrevocably. Her leg would never grow back; she was now disabled, a one-legged girl, someone that people would stare at and pity. Almost as bad in terms of Lucy's self-image was the fact that for the time being she was also reliant upon an alien attachment to her body – a plastic pouch stuck to her tummy into which she now passed poo, with no control. She earnestly prayed that this could be reversed as soon as possible. Loss of control over a basic bodily function, and having to wear a medical device to maintain a semblance of dignity, was almost more than she could bear. In the meantime she had to learn how to manage this, emptying the bag as necessary, how to change it, how to take care of the skin around it...

The anger was what saved her from serious depression. She contemplated her future – a young woman who was now disabled, one-legged, a freak (in the original sense of the word, not in the sense she had come to know as another term for a hippy), someone who would spend the rest of her life in a maimed body, able to function only with support from medical devices – first a wheelchair, later crutches, then hopefully an artificial leg, maybe a walking stick. She would never again be able to run freely, to jump out of bed, to dance... Would she ever again appear to be attractive, sexy? Would her colostomy be reversed? If it was, what scars would be left? If it wasn't, how would she cope with always having to poo into a bag on her tummy? Either way, would any man ever want her? And even if one did, would she be able to have sex satisfactorily? Lucy, although she wore glasses with quite strong lenses, had previously been considered very pretty, with her long, curly, auburn hair, blue eyes, creamy skin dusted with freckles, and cupid-bow lips, not to mention her trim figure, which curved in all the right places... But now?

Another immensely powerful emotion she went through was grief. She had experienced it before – when her father walked out of the family, and when her dog had died – and this was even more powerful; grief for the loss of the life she might have had, grief for the whole and healthy body she no longer had, grief for her leg – with the little scar on the knee where she had cut it on the ice as a toddler.

Lucy's anger and grief were effectively channelled into hard physical work, as soon as she had recovered sufficiently from the operation. Physical therapy sessions were tough and painful, but to Lucy they were not tough enough or painful enough – she wanted to physically force her bruised, battered and maimed body into submission to her will in order to be mobile.

Within a comparatively short period after Lucy's stitches were out (both from the incision in her abdomen and from her amputation), she went for rehabilitation sessions where she was fitted with a temporary prosthesis. This consisted of a cylindrical section, well-padded around the top, which fitted over her stump; attached to this was a long metal hoop, the length of the leg she had lost, with a rubber tip attached to the bottom end. A canvas strap from the cylindrical part went up crossways over Lucy's right shoulder to hold this on. On this contraption she was enabled to stand upright, and between two parallel bars she was able to take a few steps. While she could hold one of the parallel bars with her left hand, because her right arm was still in plaster, one of the therapists held her upper right arm to support her on that side. Lucy also underwent sessions with nurses regarding how to cope with and care for her stoma – how and when to empty the bag; how and when to change it; how to take care of the skin around the stoma; what to look out for regarding bleeding, infections, skin breakdown; what supplies to have with her if she was out and about; how to get supplies.

While her rehab sessions in the hospital included learning to walk with the temporary prosthesis, it was in the wheelchair she had been issued that she was discharged, to her mother's house, which created issues. The house was two-storey, her bedroom and the bathroom being upstairs. With her mother's help, she had to hop up or down the stairs. Helen Ryan, Lucy's mother, bought two items – a commode that Lucy could use downstairs if she needed to during the day, and a bath seat – basically a board that fitted across the bath, that Lucy could sit on to shower. With her right arm in plaster from knuckles to just below the elbow, bin bags had to be taped over her arm when she showered, to prevent the cast getting wet.

For some months prior to the accident she had been living in her boyfriend's flat and hanging out with a group of drop-out friends, although it was initially to her mother's home that she returned when discharged from the hospital. This posed some problems. Helen Ryan strongly disapproved of Lucy's boyfriend, Zak, but she also felt severely guilty for the accident, as it was she who had given her the motorbike. There were tensions, arguments, and tears from both of them.

Lucy tried playing her violin, even with her right wrist in plaster. It was awkward to hold the bow properly, and the cast was heavy, so to begin with she could only play for short periods, but after a bit of trial and error, she managed to do it reasonably well, and drew comfort from still being able to play.

She continued her physical therapy rehab sessions as an outpatient, doing a variety of exercises to strengthen her core, her balance, and continuing to practice walking with the cumbersome temporary prosthesis. She quickly abandoned using the wheelchair once her arm was out of plaster and she could use crutches; her wrist was still quite painful and so she kept it bandaged for another couple of weeks, so the amount of time she could spend on crutches was, at first, limited. Balance was initially an issue – her centre of balance was now considerably higher than it had been, but she quickly adjusted to this.

Lucy asked the therapists why she was issued with forearm or elbow crutches rather than axillary or underarm crutches (the longer variety, with saddles that go under the armpits). The therapists explained to her that, unless used correctly, with the saddles pressed into the sides, well below the armpits, and the weight mostly carried by the hands, long-term use of axillary crutches posed a risk of damage to the brachial plexus – the point where the nerves of the arms and hand pass through the shoulder just above the armpit – which could result in permanent nerve damage to the arms, even paralysis. Therefore the National Health Service no longer supplied axillary crutches to its patients.

Out in the world again, away from the artificially protective environment of the hospital, Lucy started to face the reality of life as an amputee. If she went out in public people stared at her. She understood this. Prior to the accident, if she had seen a young woman with only one leg, walking on crutches, she, too, would have been tempted to stare. It was nevertheless highly demoralising, reinforcing her feeling of being a freak. She also had to get used to having to reach for her crutches whenever she got out of bed, or stood up from a chair. Once, in the middle of the night, she awoke needing to pee. Half asleep, forgetting that now she had only one leg, she got up and took a step on the leg that wasn't there, only to collapse in a heap on the floor. Fortunately there was a thick carpet, and the only thing that was badly bruised was her self-esteem. Once out of the wheelchair and using crutches, she also had to get used to going up and down stairs on these, one step at a time, which took far longer than the quick ascent or descent she was used to. She also slowly got used to having the colostomy bag on her abdomen, and to emptying it and changing it as needed. One source of embarrassment for her was that it tended to make farting and gurgling noises, over which she had no control. She also had to make sure she was wearing clothing that was loose enough not to constrict the bag, or to make its shape obvious to onlookers if it started to fill while she was out and about.

She pinned a lot of her hopes, not only on having her colostomy reversed, but on an artificial leg – a prosthesis – anticipating being at least able to walk again, and to look "normal" – two-legged like everyone else. In preparation for this, as well as the sessions with the temporary prosthesis, she assiduously followed what the nurses had told her to do – bandaging her stump (the medical staff called it a residual limb, but Lucy, looking at it, saw it as a stump, thought of it as such, and always called it her stump) with wide elasticated bandages to reduce the swelling and tighten the flesh. The pain from the operation had largely gone, and the phantom limb pains had somewhat diminished, though at times they were still severe; Lucy likened them to burning electric shocks down into her missing foot. Even when these eased off, she could feel a tingling sensation like pins and needles in the toes she no longer had. Although she thought it ugly, she also gradually came to accept her stump, less than a third of her thigh, with a scar running over the end where the muscle and skin flaps had been sewn over the sawn-off bone. She tended to have nervous tremors, tics and spasms in the severed muscles, and she found that massaging her stump not only eased these but also helped reduce the severity of her phantom pains.

Eventually, the time came for her to be fitted with a proper prosthesis. In spite of herself, she found the process to be quite interesting. Her stump was wrapped in plaster-of-Paris bandages to form a mould, from which the prosthetists made a cast of her stump. On this they then fashioned a socket made of thermoplastic reinforced with fibreglass. To this, they then attached a pylon – a steel tube, with a hinged knee joint, and a moulded foot with an inflexible ankle and a rubber cushion in the heel, what the prosthetists referred to as a SACH (solid ankle cushion heel) foot. An adjustable rubber strap controlled the resistance of the knee hinge and brought the leg into a straight position when there was no resistance. Over the pylon and knee, from ankle to socket, a foam rubber cover was fitted, shaped like a leg, with a thick, approximately flesh-coloured elastic stocking over it that extended up to and over the socket. The whole thing was held on by a broad, soft leather strap that went up over Lucy's pelvis and around her waist, fastened with the new-fangled Velcro (avoiding compressing her stoma or interfering with her colostomy bag), what the prosthetists referred to as 'Silesian suspension'.

The finished prosthetic leg, when it was finally ready, felt alien, cold and impersonal and painfully uncomfortable. Weight bearing was where her pelvis, between her vulva and her remaining thigh, met the top lip of the socket, which was shaped to take the weight as evenly as possible. This meant that, although encased in stump socks and reasonably tightly held within the socket, her stump was effectively suspended, and served largely to control the forward swing of the prosthesis when she flexed her hip. A clumsy imitation of the limb she'd lost, it was a constant reminder of her disability, a stark contrast to the sense of invincibility she'd previously possessed. It was a heavy, unforgiving weight, both literally and metaphorically. Lucy initially felt deflated. The first attempts at walking, in the limb-fitting centre, again between parallel bars, were awkward and painful, punctuated by stumbles and near falls. Where the temporary prosthesis had remained straight, Lucy now had to learn to walk with a prosthesis with a knee joint, over which she had no direct control. She had to learn how, in the course of taking each and every step, she must move in such a way as to unlock the knee, swing the leg forward, let the heel strike the floor, lock the knee so it wouldn't buckle beneath her, and bring her weight over the prosthesis so that she could step forward with her real leg. Every step required concentration.

The physical therapy was gruelling, a relentless battle against her own body's betrayal. But slowly, painstakingly, she began to regain her equilibrium, her gait becoming steadier, less hesitant, and the process of taking each step slowly became automatic. However, she had – and would continue to have – a noticeable limp. From practising between the parallel bars, she moved on to walking on her prosthesis and at the same time using her crutches to ensure balance and stability. Then she progressed to using just one crutch. Slowly, she learned to trust the prosthesis, to instinctively know when the knee was locked and it would support her without giving way, and when the knee was free to flex, so she could swing it forward. She learned to incorporate it into her newfound reality, albeit reluctantly. Even when she was finally able to walk without crutches, the prosthesis was never comfortable, and wearing it for extended periods inevitably led to blisters and bruises on her stump (despite the padding provided by 'stump socks'), around her groin, where most of her weight was borne by her pelvis, and even around her waist where the belt rubbed. Burst blisters were excruciatingly painful, and putting adhesive dressings on them was difficult, as the friction that caused the blisters in the first place tended to cause the dressings to buckle or come unstuck in the hot, sweaty conditions beneath the rim of the socket. Another issue was that wearing the prosthesis for any length of time caused sweat to build up inside it. When she took it off, it stank. She had to carefully clean inside the socket with disinfectant or methylated spirit to try to eliminate this, but after some time the socket always had a faint smell even when it was clean.

Although it was supposed to look like a leg, Lucy's prosthesis didn't really fool anyone, or so it seemed to her, anyway. It looked like what it was – an artificial leg. If she got into a car, she had to lift the leg in with her hands; if she sat down, while her right foot could flex to rest flat on the floor or the ground, her artificial foot stuck out at right angles to the lower leg, so unless she was sitting on a high-seated chair only the heel rested on the ground, which made it very obvious. She found it impossible to wear flip-flops or backless sandals, as the one on the prosthetic foot continuously fell off. Fortunately for Lucy, long cotton skirts or flared jeans, with loose kaftan tops, were *de-rigeur* for 'hippy chicks' like her, and she was grateful for the fact that they hid much of the reality from public gaze, at least when she was upright. Even when, instead of wearing her prosthesis, she was on her crutches, a long skirt practically hid the absence of her leg, helping to make her feel less conspicuous and self-conscious.

On the rare occasions when Lucy was not wearing a long skirt or jeans she always wore thick tights or stockings, on both her real leg and the artificial one, which did make the latter slightly less noticeable.

Of course, her limp could not be disguised. But she hoped that most people seeing her walking simply assumed that she had suffered an injury of some sort (which, of course, she had, but not one from which she would recover and be able to walk normally).

This self-consciousness and hating being stared at was curiously tempered by the exact opposite feeling. Surreptitiously, not even admitting it to herself, Lucy felt a certain pleasure, even thrill, at going out and displaying herself as an amputee, on crutches, especially in places where no-one knew her. She couldn't begin to explain this feeling, and usually it was completely overshadowed by her more dominant feelings of wanting to hide her disability as much as possible.

Nevertheless, although there were days when Lucy was pleased with her progress, congratulated herself on her own resilience, and felt that ultimately there was little she could not achieve, there were many other days when she cried her soul out for what she had lost – the carefree, able-bodied life, where she could jump out of bed without a second thought, and run, and dance, and go to the beach in a bikini without being stared at for all the wrong reasons... But, as she knew only too well, those days could not come back, and being the realist that she was, she knew she had to accept her condition and move on with her life rather than wallow in misery, so such days gradually became fewer.

It was around this time that Lucy moved back to her erstwhile boyfriend Zak's flat, frustrated by her mother's well-meaning but suffocating concern, and her disapproval of Lucy's relationship with him. Back in his 'pad' (as he termed it) she could enjoy the effects of quite often getting stoned, without worrying that her mother would find out. She discovered that cannabis had a very therapeutic effect, both on her mood and on her physical pain.

CHAPTER TWO

Before the Crash – Part 1

✄

Lucy was born in Dublin, Ireland, on 12th March 1955, in the Rotunda Maternity Hospital in Parnell Square, near the top of O'Connell Street. Although she didn't remember much about her early life in Dublin, she and her parents lived there until she was three years old, in 1958. Then they moved to Sussex, in England, from their old house in Clontarf, North Dublin, after Lucy's father got a new job. He worked as a journalist, and had worked in the same newspaper that his father, Lucy's Grandad Ryan, had worked in for many years. Grandad Ryan was a heavy smoker, and got lung cancer and died when Lucy was two (she didn't remember him), so her father wanted to move away to a different newspaper in a different place.

After they left Dublin and arrived in Sussex they stayed in a hotel for a few weeks, but then they rented a house in a coastal town. Their furniture, which had been in storage since they left Dublin, arrived in a big van on the day they moved in, and Lucy watched with interest as the removal men unloaded and placed the furniture in the rooms where her mother, Helen, asked them to put it. Her father, Patrick, was at work in his new job.

The house was semi-detached, two-storey, with a garden, a small enclosed yard and a garage, and behind the wall of their back garden was a park. There was a pedestrian entrance into the park a little distance along the road. The house had a living room, a dining room, a kitchen, with a small enclosed yard off it, and upstairs were two reasonable-size bedrooms, a rather small room that was used as a guestroom, and a bathroom. Up again was an attic room, with walls that sloped down almost to the floor, used for storage. Lucy's parents had the room at the front. Her room looked out at the back – into the park.

Lucy's full name was Lucy Anne Ryan (actually, she was christened in church with the Irish names Luiseach Aoine, but her parents always used the anglicised versions, and these were what had been put on her birth certificate). Like the vast majority of the population of the Republic of Ireland at that time, Lucy's parents were Roman Catholic. Consequently she was baptised and brought up as a Catholic. But although, after they moved to Sussex, they attended mass in the nearest Catholic Church, her parents – especially her mother – disagreed with segregated education, and once she was old enough to attend school Lucy was enrolled in the local primary school. Her mother arranged with the parish priest that she would receive basic Catholic religious education at the church outside school hours (although he disagreed with her stance on segregated education). Lucy didn't particularly enjoy this – it made her feel different; she would rather either have gone to a Catholic primary school, like some of the other Catholic children, or not have any Catholic religious education at all. But England was not Ireland as it was at that time; attitudes to religion were much more laid back, and most other people just didn't take much notice.

Although Lucy didn't really remember a lot of her earlier life in Dublin very much, she did remember the subsequent trips the family made to visit her uncles, Sean, Liam and Colm (her father's brothers), and her Aunty Margaret (her mother's sister) – and her Granny Ryan (her father's mother) – usually at Christmas or Easter. Lucy's Uncle Liam was a Catholic priest. Her Uncles Sean and Colm were both married and had families, but her father didn't get on that well with his brothers, so Lucy didn't really get to know her paternal cousins. Her Aunty Margaret was married to a Protestant, Uncle Gerald Butler, a solicitor, and they lived in a big old house with a large garden in Foxrock, on the south-eastern outskirts of Dublin. They even had a housekeeper – which Lucy thought was very grand! They had a grown-up son, Lucy's first cousin Philip, who was at university in Cambridge, studying law like his father. Uncle Gerald had a widowed sister, Aunty Susan Patterson (Lucy called her 'Aunty' even though she was not actually directly related), and she had a son, Brian, who was almost seven years older than Lucy. Although he was no blood relation to Lucy, he was also a cousin of her cousin Philip, which she only got to work out and understand when she was a bit older. They lived on the outskirts of a small town in east County Cork, but Lucy met them in her Uncle Gerald's house. Because Uncle Gerald and Aunty Margaret had a large house, with five big bedrooms, Lucy and her parents stayed with them whenever they visited Dublin.

Lucy's mother's parents, Grandad and Granny Byrne, had left Ireland and gone to live in Boston, in America, before Lucy was born, so she didn't know them. They didn't come back to Ireland or Britain, and Lucy's parents didn't have enough money to visit them, so contact consisted of occasional letters and annual Christmas and birthday cards.

Lucy was a bit of a tomboy, and enjoyed going into the park behind their house in Sussex and climbing trees, or going to the beach, a five-minute walk from their house, and splashing in the waves. The beach was pebbles, so it wasn't any good for building sandcastles, and it was uncomfortable to walk on in bare feet, or to sit or lie on. One of Lucy's early memories was from the winter of 1959 to 1960, when ice formed on a path in the park behind the house, and she went sliding on it. Inevitably, she fell and badly gashed her left knee. Her mother, who was with her, tied her hanky round it, helped her home, and then phoned the doctor as she thought it would need stitches. She was right – the doctor put in six stitches, gave Lucy an anti-tetanus injection, and put a dressing on the wound. When it healed, the cut left a little scar across her knee.

When Lucy was about three and a half, Helen Ryan told her that she was going to have a baby, and that Lucy would have a baby brother or sister. Then, a few weeks later, Helen got ill for a few days, and became very upset, and Lucy's father, Patrick, got rather annoyed and distant. Lucy asked her mother what was wrong.

"I lost the baby," she said, tearfully.

"Well, let's try and find it," Lucy suggested, trying to be helpful. Helen explained that it didn't work like that, and that the baby had gone before it got big enough to be born. She also told Lucy that she couldn't have any more babies. So Lucy grew up as an only child, which was unusual in most Roman Catholic families at that time. Lucy later learned that this was her mother's third miscarriage, the first being before she was born, and the second before the family left Dublin, when Lucy herself was still just a baby.

When Lucy was four the family acquired a mongrel puppy called Barney. Barney was very sweet; he had a brown and white coat and soft, silky, black floppy ears, with a white muzzle and stripe up his forehead, and Lucy loved him to bits. She took him for walks in the park. At home, as a puppy, he liked to chew anything he could find, including Helen's slippers, so she had to go and buy new ones.

In September 1960, when she was five, Lucy started primary school. In school, she started to learn the alphabet, and then to read, and the children did sums (which Lucy didn't care that much about), singing, painting, and learning about other countries. Although in general Lucy enjoyed school, the teacher soon discovered that from her seat halfway back in the class, Lucy couldn't make out what was written or drawn on the blackboard. She moved Lucy up to the front, which helped, but she also sent a note to her mother saying that she thought Lucy needed to have her eyes tested.

A few days later, Helen took her to an appointment she had booked with a local optician, who tested Lucy's eyes. He seemed a nice man, with bushy grey eyebrows and a twinkle in his eyes – and he himself wore glasses, with big horn-rimmed frames. He looked into Lucy's eyes with a bright light, and then put funny-looking glasses on her, blocked out one eye and tried various lenses in front of the other, until Lucy could see his chart clearly. Then he swapped over and did the same with the other eye.

"She is short-sighted," he told Helen. "She will need glasses, which she can wear all the time for everything, and she definitely needs them for all distance viewing."

Helen tried various frames on Lucy, and ordered a pair with a mixture of brown tortoiseshell and steel. A few days later they were ready. To begin with Lucy hated them – she thought they made her look awful and she didn't like having to wear them, but at the same time she was amazed at how clearly she could see everything.

Lucy's bed was below the window in her room, and she liked to sit up in bed, pull back the curtain, and look out at the trees in the park, beyond the back garden wall. She would sometimes draw both the curtains back at night, and the trees looked like big, black, mysterious beings, silhouetted against the sky. After she got her glasses, she tried looking at the trees with and without them. Without, they were fuzzy masses; with, Lucy could clearly see every branch and twig that showed silhouetted against the sky. But it was the sky itself that most astonished her. It was full of stars. Without her glasses she could only make out the really bright ones as little fuzzy blobs of light. Now she could see thousands – maybe millions – of stars twinkling in the sky.

The next morning she told her parents excitedly, "There are millions of stars in the sky! I saw them from my bedroom window!"

Helen laughed, and hugged Lucy. "Of course there are, sweetheart."

Once she was settled in school, Patrick and Helen Ryan asked their landlord if they could now buy the house, if they took out a mortgage, to which he agreed. They also got a car, a Ford Anglia.

Helen was quite musical – she was a competent pianist, and they had a piano in their front room, which she liked to play. She was keen for Lucy to learn an instrument. Accordingly, Lucy commenced private violin and piano lessons when she was seven (Helen got her a three-quarter-size to begin with; when she was ten, she got Lucy a beautiful full-size violin with a lovely tone). Lucy was keen on music, and she practised both violin and piano assiduously. In school most of the children started to play the recorder, but the teacher, Miss Simms, knew Lucy was learning the violin and the piano. By the time she was nine, Miss Simms had Lucy playing her violin at the school concert (with herself accompanying on piano). In her early teens, Lucy also learned to play the guitar. She became quite a virtuoso on her violin, and, like her mother, a competent pianist (though she realised that on piano she would never quite be concert pianist standard!).

The winter of 1962 to 1963 was very cold, and they had quite a lot of snow. Lucy watched from her bedroom window, fascinated, as the snowflakes whirled through the air and settled in the garden and in the park beyond, coating not only the ground but every twig and branch of the trees and bushes (she had her glasses on, so she could see everything clearly). Later, she enjoyed sledging down the hill in the park.

In their house, like most people, they had a coal fire in the living room, and Lucy enjoyed sitting in front of it, eating hot buttered toast (with the butter melting). She remembered one occasion when the television was on in the corner (still in those days, of course, in black and white), but she was not really watching it. The sound was turned down. Patrick was in his armchair reading a newspaper, and Lucy was gazing into the fire, while Helen played a selection of music on the piano – Strauss waltzes, Scott Joplin rags, and Debussy's 'Girl with the Flaxen Hair'. Lucy wanted to be able to play like her mother, and this is what drove her to practise, both violin and piano. Beside Lucy, on the rug in front of the fire, Barney sat looking at her expectantly, hoping for some of her toast! She broke off a small piece and gave it to him. In less than a second it was gone.

"Barney, you won't really enjoy it if you eat it so fast," she said, and Helen laughed.

Helen took Lucy to a pantomime in Brighton – Jack and the Beanstalk. Lucy fell in love with the theatre and wanted to be an actress, as well as a musician! For a number of years afterwards Helen made a point of taking Lucy to see variety performances in the theatre on the Palace Pier in Brighton during the summer holidays (the theatre was damaged and closed in 1973), as well as pantomimes during the Christmas holidays.

About this time, all the adults that she knew became very worried by the news – something about Russia and Cuba, and missiles, and President Kennedy on the news sounding very worried about the attitude of Khruschev – none of which Lucy understood, except that whatever it was, it was serious. Then it was resolved, and everyone breathed a sigh of relief, and got on with their lives. Later on, of course, when she was older, she understood what had happened, and how close the world had come to a nuclear war.

Lucy made a number of friends at school, Mandy, Suzie, Anne, and Debbie being the main ones. They often visited one another's houses, and were invited to their various birthday parties.

In one exchange, Lucy let Mandy try on her glasses. Actually, Lucy thought Mandy looked nice wearing them, though because she herself wasn't wearing them, Mandy did look out of focus. Mandy giggled as she looked around with them on. "I can see everything clearly with them except close-to," she said, waggling her fingers in front of her face, "but they make everything look a little smaller and a little curved in at the edges, like one of those round mirrors with a curved surface."

"Convex," Lucy said, showing off her vocabulary. She had noticed this effect herself, like a fisheye lens, when she first wore her glasses, but she had become so used to wearing them all the time that now everything just looked normal to her. It was when she took them off that things became blurry and out of focus.

Lucy was not into dolls. She did have a couple of teddy bears that she liked cuddling – especially in bed – but she mostly enjoyed reading books, drawing and painting pictures, riding her bicycle and playing with Barney – apart, of course, from playing her violin and the piano.

In the summer, the Ryan family went for a weekend in London to see the sights and do some shopping. Later in the same summer, they went on a five-day trip to Dublin to visit Lucy's Granny Ryan and her uncles and aunt. They travelled by train to London Victoria, by Underground to Euston, by train to Holyhead in North Wales, and by ferry from Holyhead to Dun Laoghaire, south of Dublin. The journey lasted a whole day. Uncle Gerald met them with his car at the ferry terminal in Dun Laoghaire.

Lucy enjoyed reading in bed; sometimes she got so engrossed in a book that Helen had to come and tell her to sleep, and turn the light off. Lucy even sometimes tried reading by torchlight under the bedclothes! However, this had the consequence that, if the next day was a weekday during the school term, she found it difficult to wake up the next morning, and could not concentrate in class. Although she was short-sighted, which meant without her glasses she couldn't see distant objects clearly, as time passed she didn't bother taking off her glasses to read, unless for some reason she held the book quite close or the print was very small. And every few years, after getting her eyes tested again, she would have to get new glasses, sometimes with slightly stronger lenses.

Another of Lucy's keen interests was, of course, listening to music. The Ryans had a radiogram (a combination of radio and record player – very 1960s!) in the sitting room, and over the years they acquired a sizeable collection of records covering a wide variety of music. Patrick liked Irish traditional music, folk music, jazz, and crooners like Frank Sinatra and Bing Crosby. Helen preferred classical music and what would generally be described as 'light' music, including things like songs from musicals. On the radio they listened to all three BBC radio stations – the Home Service (which later became Radio 4), the Light Programme (which became Radio 2) and the Third Network (later renamed Radio 3). Sometimes Patrick would also tune in to Radio Athlone for what he liked to term "a taste of home". Although the BBC Home Service was primarily a channel for drama, news, current affairs, magazine programmes, quizzes and – for children – *Listen with Mother*, even the latter added to Lucy's musical education as at the end of the programme each day, the closing music was a piece of piano music that Helen told Lucy was the *Berceuse* from Fauré's *Dolly Suite*. This was just one of a number of signature tunes on the radio that Lucy absorbed during this period, including *Barwick Green* by Arthur Wood (theme tune of *The Archers*), *Horse Guards* by Haydn Wood (*Down Your Way*), The *Clog Dance* from *La Fille mal gardée* by Heróld (*Home This Afternoon*), and Eric Coates' *By the Sleepy Lagoon* (*Desert Island Discs*).

As well as the Cuban Missile Crisis, Lucy was also aware of other things happening in the world during this part of her childhood, although none of them affected her directly – the assassination of President Kennedy, the death and state funeral of Sir Winston Churchill (which they watched on their black-and-white television), and England winning the football World Cup.

During the course of Lucy's early childhood she had the usual range of childhood illnesses – chicken pox, mumps, German measles, and sometimes colds and sore throats, or tummy upsets, but she was generally a healthy child, and recovered quickly from most things.

When Lucy was eight, she made her first communion. Helen got her a gorgeous white satin and lace dress and veil, with little white shoes and a dainty white handbag. Lucy was much more interested in these than she was in the white missal Granny Ryan gave her, or in the service itself, though she enjoyed being given sweets and treats afterwards. She now considered herself a fully-fledged Catholic, and didn't feel she needed to continue attending her extra-curricular religious education sessions, and she pressured her parents into stopping them, provided she attended mass regularly and went to confession once a month. Patrick, although he was brought up a strict Catholic, and his brother Liam was a priest, didn't really care either way, and Helen agreed somewhat reluctantly, but she had other things on her mind.

Patrick and Helen Ryan by this time were having frequent heated arguments, usually about Patrick drinking or staying out very late at night, and about money. Things had been gradually getting tense between them for quite some time – probably since they took out the mortgage to buy the house. But now the situation was getting steadily worse, and Lucy felt upset and scared of what might happen. She remembered one night hearing them shouting at each other. Helen accused her husband not only of being drunk, and of spending the money she needed for food and housekeeping, but of having another woman. Lucy didn't know what she meant, but could tell by the heated voices that it was very bad. The next day Patrick was late to breakfast – it was a weekend, so he didn't have to go to work. He looked awful, and complained of a headache.

"Patrick, you have only yourself to blame," Helen exclaimed, banging a mug of black coffee in front of him and stomping into the kitchen. She usually called him 'Pat'. For her to call him 'Patrick' meant she was very angry and upset with him.

"Daddy, have you got another woman?" Lucy innocently asked.

"Oh, Sacred Heart of God! Not you, too!" He, in turn, got up and stomped out of the room. A few minutes later, Lucy heard the front door bang as he went out.

Later on – Lucy wasn't sure if it was the same day or a day or two later – she found her mother in the living room looking distraught. She had clearly been crying, and her eyes were red.

"It's Daddy, isn't it?" Lucy asked. She gulped, and nodded. "Mummy, what does it mean, that he has another woman?"

Helen looked aghast. "Who told you that?"

"I heard you saying it to Daddy."

"Sweetheart, you weren't meant to hear that."

"But what does it mean?"

"I think it means that Daddy doesn't love me anymore, and that he's found someone else to spend his time with, that he loves more than me."

"Does that mean he doesn't love me anymore too?" Lucy remembered how he had said, '*Oh Sacred Heart of God! Not you too!*' and left the room, clearly very angry.

"I don't know, darling." Helen burst into fresh tears.

This anger between them got worse, not better, and a couple of weeks later they had an almighty row which ended with Patrick throwing most of his clothes and things into a couple of suitcases, and storming out, driving away in the car – the Ford Anglia, their family car! He didn't come back.

Lucy didn't know what to think about her father leaving them. Of course, she loved him, and she was very upset. But the fact that he left – without even saying goodbye to her – made her wonder if he didn't love her anymore. Helen was extremely upset, not just because she had loved him, and then he started drinking and cheating on her, with horrific rows, but also because, in all practical ways, her entire world had virtually collapsed. She had come to Sussex and built her life here because of him. He had fathered her child – Lucy. Now she was left, high and dry. They were living in a house with mortgage payments still to be met, but no pay from Patrick Ryan to pay them. And, of course, being Catholic, divorce was out of the question. Helen did find a solicitor, and, having been until then a 'housewife', started looking urgently for a job.

Lucy wasn't aware of all the ramifications – issues of maintenance, of house ownership and whether they would have to sell, or if her father would agree to sell his fifty-percent share to her mother, and how Helen would pay for it, or all the other things Helen had to cope with, but Lucy did know for quite a period that her mother was very worried that they might end up losing the house. For her part, Lucy was upset both because her father had left, and because her mother was upset. She also felt less sure of her place in the scheme of things, less secure in her family. Although she still had her mother and Barney, she wondered if circumstances could suddenly sweep them away too. For a period her schoolwork suffered, and she became moody and tearful. But her nature was such that she quickly bounced back.

There were also issues of discrimination against Irish people. Lucy had discovered some of this in school. Although she had lost her Irish accent, her surname was enough for some of the children to realise she was Irish and taunt her with it. Obviously, looking back later, Lucy realised that their attitudes must have come from their parents. This was in the era when some boarding houses in England had signs in their windows – 'No dole, no blacks, no Irish'. So Helen, who still had a soft Dublin accent, would have faced discrimination.

Despite this, Helen managed to get a good job as an office administrator, made sure the mortgage payments went in on time, and after a bit, the issue over title deeds was sorted between her solicitor and another solicitor representing Patrick. Because they had only owned the house for a relatively short period, Lucy learned later that her father's equity in the house was not too great, and somehow Helen managed to buy him out and maintain the mortgage (many years later she learned that her Uncle Gerald had helped Helen financially at this time). She also managed to buy a second-hand Morris Minor, so they had transport again. But they had to scrimp and save in lots of other ways. They didn't eat out, didn't often go to the cinema or theatre, and Lucy's birthday and Christmas presents were usually inexpensive.

Of course the fact that Helen was out at work every day (Monday to Friday) meant that Lucy was a 'latch-key' child – she would arrive home from school to find only Barney in the house until her mother got in a couple of hours later (Barney would have access to the enclosed yard, which they kept locked from the garden). Lucy often used this time to play with Barney and take him for walks in the park. Occasionally, after school, she would visit a friend's house, but didn't like leaving Barney on his own for too long, when he had been left all day as it was.

Less than a year after Patrick left, Helen told Lucy that he had been in touch to say that he and his new partner were moving to Australia (his partner was Australian). So that was that. Lucy afterwards got cards and a little money sent from him for birthdays and Christmas, but little other contact for many years.

About this time, Lucy began to have an idea of where babies come from. She asked her mother, and Helen told her that most species of plants and animals have males and females, and in order to reproduce, the males have to fertilise the females. In plants this is mostly done by pollen being transferred from a male flower to the reproductive part of a female flower – by insects such as bees or by the wind. In animals, it is done mostly by contact between a male and female, and in mammals – of which humans are a species – this involves the male animal's penis entering the female animal's vagina and 'ejaculating' (squirting!) sperm, which then travels to the uterus (womb) and potentially fertilises one or more eggs, which then develop into foetuses (unborn babies). Helen explained that, in humans, because children require a long-term commitment to raise them, it is usual for a man and woman to get married and provide a lasting environment for bringing up children. Lucy was, of course, fairly aware from her religious education what the Catholic Church's teachings were on marriage and children, and acutely conscious that her father had, in effect, abrogated his parental responsibilities.

Lucy took this information on board and realised that when she saw birds mating in the park (or dogs, come to that), this was what they were doing. She found a picture in a book of Michelangelo's statue of David, and was fascinated by what was between his legs. Of course, she had seen small boys when they were naked, but never a grown man. She wondered how something that was so obviously floppy (even though on the statue it was made of marble and therefore very hard) could go into the relevant part of a female!

CHAPTER THREE

Brian – Early Life, Part One

✄

Brian Edmund Patterson was born on 8th July 1948 in Bombay, India, son of Major Dermott and Mrs Susan Patterson. Dermott, like his wife, was of Anglo-Irish stock – his father had been a doctor in Dublin until 1940, and died of a heart attack in 1946. By 1948, Dermott was a trade representative for an Anglo-Indian wholesale firm that did two-way trade in a variety of goods – textiles, spices, ceramics, furniture and luxury goods in the newly independent India. However, his health was not good. He had been an officer in the British Army during the war, had fought in various theatres of war, and had been badly wounded during the Ardennes campaign – the 'Battle of the Bulge', where he had suffered leg and facial injuries. Although he largely recovered from his injuries (he walked with a stiff-legged limp, and he was blind in one eye), he suffered severe post-traumatic stress – what used to be termed 'shell shock'. In 1950 he caught a fever and had to be hospitalised for a month. On discharge from hospital he was too weak and emaciated to return to work for many weeks, as a result of which the firm he worked for laid him off. The family returned to Ireland – to Susan's family home in County Cork. Dermott's health continued to suffer, both mentally and physically, and increasingly he lived on cigarettes, drink, and tranquilisers. He developed lung cancer and died in 1956, at the age of only forty-two.

Susan had inherited a private income. Her parents had also died quite young, and by the time she and Dermott returned to Ireland, with two-year-old Brian, she was the owner of not only the family home in County Cork, but also the income from the capital her father had gained by selling off the family estate in 1935. It was on this income that the family lived.

Brian remembered virtually nothing of India, except vague memories of his *ayah* (Indian nanny), and of a sunny garden full of trees and bushes with brightly coloured and sweet-smelling flowers – hibiscus, bougainvillea, and frangipani, and the smell of spices from the kitchen. However, as he grew he read avidly about India, and longed to go back and see something of the country.

Ireland was very different. It rained a lot, and although the countryside was very green, it was a soft and muted green. The winters were cold and damp; the summers varied between cool and damp and warm and occasionally sunny.

Ireland in the 1950s and 1960s was quite an insular place, very conservative in its culture, which was dominated by the Roman Catholic Church. There was no divorce, no contraceptives, strict moral censorship on books, films, and plays, and most of the population – both Catholic and Protestant – went to church every Sunday. The economy, outside the two largest cities (Dublin and Cork) was largely rural – agriculture, fishing, and forestry. Many people still had memories of the 'War of Independence' (the IRA campaign that commenced with the Easter Rising of 1916 and culminated in the Anglo-Irish Treaty of 1921, which granted autonomy to 26 of the 32 counties that comprised Ireland, forming the 'Irish Free State'), and the bitter civil war that followed (between those who accepted the treaty, and those who wanted to continue the campaign for total independence). Although both sides had reconciled, and the country had been a fully independent republic since 1949, the differences were still reflected in the two largest political parties, Fianna Fail (which was formed by Eamon de Valera from most of the anti-treaty elements) and Fine Gael (from the pro-treaty elements).

Brian grew up in a big old Georgian house, with five bedrooms, drawing room, study, dining room, kitchen and pantry, a conservatory and a range of outbuildings. The furniture, too, was old – mahogany wardrobes, chests, tables and chairs, big oil paintings of landscapes in muted colours on the walls, interspersed with prints of hunting and horse-racing scenes.

Brian's parents were Protestants – Church of Ireland. The Protestant population of the local area was quite small, and formed a fairly tight-knit community, surrounded as they were by the much larger Roman Catholic population. They were mostly well-to-do members of either the landed gentry or the professional classes. However, Susan was not at all stand-offish, was liberal in her views, and had as many Catholic friends as she did Protestant ones. However, in the 1950s there were no mixed-denomination schools in the Republic of Ireland, and mixed marriages were often frowned upon (by both communities).

Brian therefore started, in September 1953, in a Church of Ireland run primary school, which he attended until June 1958. He then went to a fee-paying preparatory school in Dublin, as a boarder, for three years before proceeding to a boarding college (secondary school – what in England would be termed a 'Public School', i.e. a fee-paying private school).

Despite having segregated schooling, because Susan had Catholic friends, some of whom also had children of roughly the same age as Brian, he had a number of friends of his age group who were Catholic and went mostly to National Schools under the aegis of the Catholic Church.

Although these were mostly boys, one was a girl called Cathy (her full first name was Catriona), whose mother often met Susan for morning coffee. She was three months older than Brian, had two younger sisters and a younger brother, and was very pretty with long, silky blonde hair and big blue eyes. She had caught polio when she was a baby, before inoculations became widely available. As a result, she was left with her right leg paralysed and had to wear a steel calliper, or leg brace, with brown leather straps and buckles. Some of the other kids at Cathy's school teased her about her leg, and one day Brian found her limping home in tears, so he tried to comfort her. Her limp reminded him of the way his father walked. This cemented their friendship and, because all her siblings were younger, outside of school he became her protector. Except for the teasing Cathy wasn't bothered about her disability – she didn't remember not being that way, so she was completely used to it; what bothered her was being different and being teased by others because she was different.

Cathy and Brian had childish discussions with each other about what the other's religion entailed. Brian's description of Morning Prayer and Holy Communion sounded to Cathy very similar to a Catholic mass, except that mass was said in Latin (at that time; it was changed in the 1960s to the vernacular under *Vatican II*), while the Church of Ireland service was in English. The big differences seemed to be that Catholic priests didn't marry, Protestant ones did; Catholics went to confession, Protestants didn't; although in both churches children got confirmed at about the same age (13 or 14), Catholics made their first communion at about 8 or 9 years of age, Church of Ireland children only when they were confirmed; Catholics said the rosary, Protestants didn't, and Catholics could eat fish but no meat on Fridays (also done away with by *Vatican II*), Protestants didn't have any fast day. At that age, they had no real conception of dogma or theological differences and didn't know that, apart from the Church of Ireland (part of the Anglican Church), there were many other denominations of Protestants, and indeed, Christian churches that were neither Catholic nor Protestant (such as Orthodoxy).

Later, in his teenage years, Brian questioned his religion and eventually came to the view that, while God might exist, and spirituality was a desirable trait, religion tended to divide people more than anything, except possibly politics and race, and thereafter he only attended religious services as a token of respect for his mother, or because it was a compulsory part of his schooling.

One Friday afternoon, after Brian came out from school, being met by Susan, they happened to meet Cathy as she came out of her school, and he asked Susan if Cathy could come over to their house for tea, so Susan spoke to Cathy's mother and she agreed that Cathy could go with Brian and Susan, and she would collect her at seven o'clock in the evening. Brian got into the back of the car, and Cathy got into the front passenger seat, unlocking the knee hinges on her calliper as she did so. When they got to Brian's home, he took Cathy up to his bedroom (she had to come up the stairs slowly, one step at a time), and she showed Brian her calliper in detail. The leather straps had buckles and went around her leg at the upper thigh, just above and just below her knee, and just above her ankle. At the knee, the hinges locked when her leg was straightened, and she had to unlock them again by lifting a small steel bar if she wanted her knee to bend when she sat down. Over her knee was a wide brown leather cover, with a circular cloth pad over her kneecap. This held her knee in place and prevented it from bending forwards when the knee hinges were locked. The bottom of the calliper had strong springs at the ankle, and it fitted into slots in the heel of the built-up sole of the special shoe she wore on her right foot (the sole was about one inch thicker than the normal shoe on her left). She told Brian it was called an orthotic shoe. Her foot was held at right angles to her leg, unless she put pressure on the toes, in which case the springs at the ankle would allow some movement.

"What happens if you don't wear your calliper?" Brian asked.

"I can hop on my left leg," she said. "But if I try and stand or walk on my right leg, I just fall down. I can move my hip, but further down

I can't hold it straight, or bend the knee, it just hangs there and drags."

"Does your leg hurt?"

"No. It doesn't feel very much. It's sort of semi-numb. Mummy is always checking to make sure that the straps of my calliper aren't too tight. She thinks they might cut off the blood, or cause sores that I might not feel."

She took her calliper off, to show Brian how it worked. Her right leg was much thinner than the left, especially below the knee, as the muscles had atrophied. It was also over one inch shorter than her left leg – hence the built-up sole on her orthotic shoe. She allowed Brian to feel her leg; it was limp and the joints were rather floppy.

On another occasion, in the spring, Cathy came to the Pattersons' house on a Saturday afternoon, and after they had listened to children's programmes on the radio (at that time Susan hadn't yet acquired a television), they went into the garden, which was quite big and had several trees. Brian started to climb a tree. Cathy tried to join in, but because of her leg she found it impossible on her own, and Brian had to help her up into one of the easier trees.

"I never climbed a tree before," Cathy said, happy and excited.

Getting her down again was even trickier. She could not, of course, jump, so Brian had to climb down and give her a hand to get down from the fairly low branch she had managed to get to, letting her land on the ground on her good leg while Brian caught her and prevented her from falling.

These events took place while Brian's father, Dermott, was still alive, but in and out of hospital, first in Cork, then in Dublin, and wasting away. Brian knew he was dying. At home, Dermott eventually took to his bed, and remained there. The doctor called frequently, and Susan spent a lot of time physically nursing him. One morning, when he was eight, Brian noticed his father's bedroom door was shut when he got up, and remained so until he went to school (by that time, he was making his own way to school). When he returned home in the afternoon, he found Susan sitting in the study, in tears.

"Oh," he said. "I suppose Dad has died."

"Yes, dear," Susan replied, tearfully.

While Brian was saddened, he was not exactly devastated. He loved his father, but Dermott had been slowly dying for years, so it was no surprise. It had been a long time since father and son had played together, or had much meaningful interaction. So Brian's feelings were of sorrow, rather than grief, and if anything he was more upset that his mother was grief-stricken, though she did her best to put a brave face on it.

CHAPTER FOUR

Before the Crash – Part Two

H elen Ryan's financial situation gradually got better, and in the summer of 1964, when Lucy was nine, having put Barney in boarding kennels, Lucy and Helen flew over to Cork. It was Lucy's first flight. They stayed for a week with 'Aunty Susan' and Brian, who was now sixteen, before spending a couple of nights with Lucy's Uncle Gerald and Aunty Margaret in Dublin on the way home. In County Cork they visited Youghal, where Brian showed Lucy an old Elizabethan house called 'Myrtle Grove', where Sir Walter Raleigh had lived. Aunty Susan had a comfortable old Georgian house full of antique furniture. There was a grandfather clock in the hall, which chimed the hours, and made a nice 'tick-tock' sound. Lucy liked opening the door and watching the pendulum swing to and fro. She had heard the song *My Grandfather's Clock*, and this one always made her think of it.

Lucy felt her mother and Aunty Susan got on so well together because in some ways they were in a similar situation. Aunty Susan's husband, Dermott, had been an officer in the British Army, badly wounded during the Ardennes campaign and though he largely recovered, found life in India too stressful and increasingly lived on cigarettes, drink, and tranquilisers. Even after the family returned to Ireland, his health deteriorated, he developed lung cancer, and died in 1956, aged only forty-two. So Aunty Susan was left a widow, with a young son to raise, while Helen Ryan was left as an abandoned wife with a young daughter to raise.

In due course Lucy did her 'eleven plus', and passed, so she started at grammar school in 1966. The only one of Lucy's primary school friends who went to the same school was Mandy, although by now she wasn't Lucy's closest friend.

Before she started at grammar school, Brian and Aunty Susan came over from Ireland and stayed with Helen and Lucy in the summer, and the four of them went on holiday together to the Isle of Man. Barney went into kennels, and they got trains to London and then to Liverpool and boarded the ferry to Douglas (Lucy's first time on a ship, and she was very excited). They stayed in a hotel on the seafront in Douglas, and enjoyed the horse trams, the Snaefell Electric Mountain Railway (they had tea in the café at the summit of Snaefell, and admired the view in all directions, as England, Scotland, Ireland, and Wales were all visible), the steam trains to Port Erin (where there was a nicer beach than in Douglas), and listening to a band in the Villa Marina Gardens. Between them, the two mothers hired a car for a few days and they explored the island, touring the TT motorbike racing circuit, going to the Big Wheel at Laxey, to Peel (which had a better beach than Douglas, and with a lovely old ruined castle on the headland overlooking the bay), Castletown (another old castle – Castle Rushen – but not a ruin), and Point of Ayr (a lighthouse at the northern tip of the island). They also saw a few Manx cats – which didn't have tails. Their week on the island passed quickly, and before they knew it they were on the ferry and then the train home again, but looking forward to collecting Barney. Aunty Susan and Brian returned to Ireland.

At grammar school, Lucy did okay. She was good at English, art, geography, history, music, domestic science, French, and Spanish, and she was okay but not brilliant at maths and science subjects. Lucy was never a very sporty girl. For one thing, most sports involved removing her glasses, and she had now come to rely on them and hated taking them off, as everything immediately went out of focus. Over the years, her short-sightedness had gradually increased. Her very first glasses, when she was five, had a strength of minus 1.5 dioptres. By the time she was thirteen, her prescription was minus 3.75 dioptres for her right eye and minus 4.00 for her left. Without her glasses Lucy could only see things really clearly a few inches in front of her face, everything else was just blurry, so she wore her glasses from the time she woke up until she went to sleep, except when she was in the shower or swimming. Her Granny Ryan wore thick glasses with lenses like bottle bottoms, and her father wore glasses, so she felt perhaps she had inherited her myopia from them.

Anyway, she did play a bit of tennis (keeping her glasses on – Billie-Jean King, who wore glasses, was her tennis idol), and she was also quite a good swimmer. Her chief interests were music, painting and drawing, riding her bicycle, and reading. She still occasionally climbed trees in the park.

It was at about the age of thirteen when Lucy had her first period. Her mother (she called her 'Mum' now, rather than 'Mummy') bought Lucy her first sanitary towels, though she subsequently preferred to use tampons. Lucy's breasts were also growing rapidly – actually becoming quite big for her size – and she now wore bras all the time.

Lucy started to take an interest in boys. By now, of course, she was aware of the mechanics of sex. She started to fantasise about making love, and sometimes at night, in bed, she felt herself, and rubbed her finger between her labia. It got her quite excited, and she found that the little piece of flesh just at the opening of her vulva – her clitoris – got enlarged and stiff, and it felt fantastic when she touched it when it was like this. However, Catholic schoolgirl that she was, she felt guilty, as she knew that in doing this, masturbating, she was committing a sin according to Catholic doctrine (which, although she sometimes questioned it in her mind, she still largely believed)!

Lucy started looking at boys, mostly the ones in her school. And she noticed that some of them looked quite admiringly at her. She supposed that she was quite pretty – several people told her she was. Of course, she thought her glasses, with their quite strong lenses, made her look terrible, but she was unable to function without them and could not bear the thought of putting contact lenses in her eyes. Lucy wasn't very tall, but she was slim and was curving in all the right places, especially her breasts! She had very long, curly hair of a rich auburn colour (her mother's hair was a natural blonde, and her father had deep red hair), her eyes were blue, she had an oval face with a pert nose, and quite full lips. Her skin was creamy, dusted with freckles (which she didn't like), but at least she only got a few spots, unlike some of the other girls in her class who had full-blown acne. Lucy had a little brown mole just below her right eye, which she would rather not have had. She had a few other moles, some slightly bigger, in other places, too – two on her abdomen just above the pubic hair, which her body was now growing, and one close to the areola around the nipple of her left breast. She thought her teeth and gums showed rather too much when she smiled, and she wasn't sure her teeth were absolutely straight.

In her early teens, Lucy was not a particularly rebellious teenager, though she supposed on reflection that she and her mother had their share of disagreements, usually over things like homework, staying out late, and clothes. None of these disagreements were particularly serious, and over the important things Lucy usually ended up accepting her mother's greater wisdom and experience, even when she didn't want to comply. In things that weren't so important, Helen usually tried to see Lucy's perspective and either give way or settle for a compromise. But overall, Lucy respected the difficulties her mother had faced with her father's behaviour and his subsequent departure, and how she had coped and done the best she could for Lucy.

It was in her mid-teens that Lucy went on a four-day school trip to France, visiting Paris, Versailles, and Calais. On her return, Helen met Lucy from ferry in Dover. She looked upset.

"Mum, what's wrong?"

"It's Barney. He's old, and very sick, and I don't think he will last much longer. I took him to the vet on Tuesday, but there was nothing he could do. He just said that I should make him comfortable. He offered to put him to sleep, but he said it wouldn't make much difference – that Barney would probably be gone in a few days anyway, and he's not in extreme pain."

This immediately put a dampener on Lucy's high spirits from her trip to France. She loved Barney dearly – he had been a faithful little companion to her for most of her childhood, always sweet-tempered, always glad to see her, wagging his tail and looking at her with his big soft eyes, licking her hands or face when he got the chance.

They arrived home, and for the first time that Lucy could remember since they got him, Barney didn't come to the door to greet them. She dumped her bag in the hall and went into the living room, where Barney had his bed. He was lying in it, but looked up as she entered, and gently wagged his tail. His eyes had a misty, faraway look.

"Oh, Barney," she said, and got down on the floor beside him. She caressed him, and he licked her hand. She stroked his silky ears, and kissed the top of his head. His tail continued to wag weakly. Then, after some time, he lifted his head, looked at Lucy, gave a little whimper, and breathed out with a sigh, sinking back into his bed, and was still. There was no more breath, and his tail was now motionless. He had held on to say goodbye to her, and now he had gone.

Lucy was in bits. She and her mother cried, trying to comfort each other, and just cried more.

The next day, Lucy and Helen buried Barney in the garden, close to the wall of the park where Lucy had taken him for countless walks, and later, they bought a rose bush and planted it over him.

Helen and Lucy had occasional visits from Brian in the following couple of years. He was at Oxford, reading medicine, and Helen knew that Susan was intensely proud of him.

It was around this time that the problems of being Irish in England were exacerbated by the increasing levels of violence in Northern Ireland. This was the start of the so-called 'Troubles', which would subsequently continue for many years. Northern Ireland was part of the UK, but had its own government that maintained policies more than somewhat biased against Catholics, who mostly wanted a united Ireland. A civil rights movement to protest this bias and discrimination was met with rejection, and violence broke out, with Republican men of violence (the IRA) commencing their campaign of bombing and shooting, particularly against the British Army and the police, but in which many civilians also suffered. Then, of course, Loyalist paramilitary groups (the UVF and the UDA) took up arms against the Republicans, and again innocent people also suffered. Lucy didn't really understand all the political arguments, but she did understand that anyone with Irish roots or connections was regarded with increased suspicion, if not outright hostility, in England.

This didn't impact too much on Lucy as far as school was concerned. In music classes she was the teacher's star pupil (she had private violin and piano lessons as well as doing music in school). The highlight of this came with the school concert in the early summer of 1970. Lucy, aged sixteen, had a starring role, playing Vaughan Williams' *The Lark Ascending*, accompanied by Mrs Grant, the music teacher, on piano. She had spent several months learning and practising this piece (with a lot of help from her violin and piano teacher, Mr Scott), and although her performance was not absolutely fault-free, she received a standing ovation from the audience of parents, teachers, and other pupils. Of course she was over the moon, and on an absolute high for some days afterwards. She was also learning the *Czardas* by Monti – a violin piece full of virtuosic fireworks, based on gypsy music.

By the time of this concert, Lucy had become a much more independent and, in some ways, rebellious teenager. Apart from music and English, she had come to dislike school, largely because she was being bullied by some of the other girls. Although it wasn't obvious, Lucy knew that this was primarily because of three things – she was Irish, she was Catholic, and her parents had split up. She couldn't do anything about any of this – except renounce her Catholic faith, which increasingly she was willing to do. While she believed in God, she had increasingly come to question the moral teachings of the Catholic Church, and even as far as Christianity was concerned she became very sceptical. Having earlier in her teens gone through a period when she became quite religious – spending a lot of time on her knees in her bedroom in front of either her crucifix or her small china statue of the Virgin Mary praying, and thinking of becoming a nun (which, to the young teenage Lucy – after watching *The Sound of Music*, seemed quite a glamorous vocation), she had since thought more deeply about this and questioned everything. She knew Christianity taught that only through belief in Jesus could a person attain Heaven, but to Lucy this seemed grossly unfair to the millions of people who either never heard of Jesus, or who were simply brought up in other faiths and religions – or none.

Helen, herself a committed Catholic (despite her opposition to segregated education), viewed her daughter's increasing scepticism about her religion with concern, and it led to some arguments.

Bullying at school was an issue that, at that time, could not be discussed with teachers – or indeed, most adults. For one thing, there was a 'code of honour' amongst schoolchildren that, no matter what happened to you, you did not 'sneak' – or tell adults, especially not teachers. Amongst many adults, who had gone through the process in their own schooldays, there was often an attitude that bullying was good to toughen one up, to build character, and that one should learn to keep a stiff upper lip.

Irrespective of actually ceasing to practise Catholicism, the bullying at school was based on perception, and declaring that she was no longer a practising Catholic would not have made any difference. The bullying that Lucy experienced took a number of forms: she was ostracised by some of her schoolmates – 'sent to Coventry' as it was termed; her school books were sometimes defaced when she wasn't looking; very occasionally she was physically attacked – pinched, scratched, slapped and spat at; more frequently she was subject to cutting remarks or name calling.

Another bone of contention between Lucy and her mother was that Lucy decided she wanted to be vegetarian. Her mother, who had always happily cooked and eaten meat and fish, couldn't understand this, and failed miserably to provide appetising vegetarian meals, so Lucy, through trial and error, taught herself to cook reasonably tasty and nutritious meals with no meat or fish ingredients. Eating out was slightly more problematic. While most Indian restaurants provided a selection of vegetarian dishes, and Italian pizzerias usually had either margherita pizzas, with just a tomato and cheese topping, or mushroom pizzas, British vegetarian restaurants at that time were hard to find, and those that did exist were usually 'wholefood' restaurants that offered dishes such as nut roast, lentil and vegetable pies made with wholewheat pastry, and brown rice with aduki beans and steamed vegetables. While such meals were, no doubt, healthy, Lucy did not find them particularly appetising.

Her musical tastes had also broadened. While she still loved classical music and played it on her violin, Lucy listened to records by many pop bands, especially The Beatles. She was fascinated by their advocacy of both psychedelic drugs and Hindu mysticism.

Because of the bullying, Lucy would frequently arrive home in tears and her mother exhibited sufficient sympathy, insight, and understanding that she realised something needed to be done. A friend of Helen's told her that her own son was doing his 'O' levels at the local technical college, and Helen asked Lucy if she would like to leave school and attend the 'tech' to continue her studies. Lucy jumped at the suggestion.

The only downside to doing her 'O' and 'A' levels at the 'tech' was that they didn't do music. Here, however, Lucy's violin and piano teacher, Mr Scott, stepped into the breach. Lucy explained the problem. He offered to give her music theory lessons as well as her instrumental lessons, and to enrol her privately for 'O' and 'A' level music exams as well as her grade exams in violin and piano when the time came (Grade 8 for violin, Grade 7 for piano).

To compensate to some extent for what Lucy had gone through in school, Helen acquired tickets for one of the Promenade Concerts in the Royal Albert Hall in London, staying overnight in a hotel. They travelled up to London by train, and of course both thoroughly enjoyed the concert.

CHAPTER FIVE

Brian – Early Life, Part Two

※

Brian detested his prep school. When he started there, it was his first time away from home, and he was very homesick. The routine was regimented, the meals were awful, some of the masters (the teachers – all men, and they all wore black gowns) were very strict and severe (Brian termed them ante-diluvian), and corporal punishment was frequent and administered for any misdemeanour. But the worst part of it all was the fact that bullying was rife. Some of the bigger boys picked on Brian, calling him a mummy's boy, picking fights with him, and generally trying to get him into trouble. If a fight was caught by the teachers, the victim got caned as well as the perpetrator. There was, of course, the usual code of conduct amongst the boys that, whatever injustices they inflicted on each other, it was absolutely forbidden to 'sneak' – to tell a teacher or any of the adult staff. A sneak was regarded as the absolute lowest of the low. The only redeeming aspects of life in the prep school for Brian were that he was good academically and enjoyed learning, and that he could run fast and was therefore sometimes chosen as wing three quarter for the rugby team for his year (during the Christmas and Easter terms), and for the cricket team (during the summer term). The kudos of this did help to dimmish the bullying, and as he progressed and got bigger it had virtually ceased by the time he left his prep school.

Although Susan remained on friendly terms with Cathy's mother, after Brian went to boarding school he rather lost touch with Cathy.

During the school holidays, Brian occasionally saw her about the town and they would say, "Hi," to each other, but that was about it. Cathy still wore a calliper on her paralysed leg, and her orthotic shoe now had a three-inch thick sole, as her paralysed leg didn't grow quite as much as the other. On one occasion they went for an ice cream together, and had a conversation to catch up. Cathy told Brian that, although her parents didn't agree with her, as soon as she was old enough to authorise the decision herself she wanted to have her leg amputated above the knee, as she considered an artificial leg would give her a better appearance and better function. To Brian, while it sounded rather drastic, he understood her reasoning. Her shortened, atrophied, and practically useless leg was not much good to her, and her calliper made her disability very obvious.

Then her parents moved to another part of Ireland, and Brian saw no more of her.

It was at Easter 1960 (Easter Sunday was 17th April), when Brian was eleven, rising twelve, during his Easter holidays from boarding school, that he and his mother went to Dublin and stayed with his Uncle Gerald Butler (Susan's brother) and his wife, Aunty Margaret (who was a Catholic). Brian's Aunty Margaret's sister Helen, brother-in-law Patrick, and five-year-old daughter Lucy were also staying there. Lucy was a pretty child, with curly reddish-bronze hair, and she was a bit of a tomboy. Despite the age gap, Brian quite enjoyed playing with her in his uncle's big garden at their house in Foxrock, south of Dublin.

This was the first of several times over the next few years that Brian saw Lucy and her mother. The next time, a couple of years later, Patrick had left Helen, so he wasn't there. By that time Lucy was wearing glasses, which Brian initially thought rather gawky, but then he decided that they quite suited her.

He found that college was both similar and different from his prep school. It was still a boarding school and there was still a certain amount of bullying, though not as overtly belligerent as at prep school, but the food, though still not great, was somewhat better, and the teaching staff (although still mostly male, dressed in black gowns, and called masters) were generally less severe and more interested in developing their pupils than in imposing an autocracy. Brian continued to do well academically and in both rugby and cricket, and so fared reasonably well. He completed his Junior Certificate in June 1964, shortly before his sixteenth birthday. By this stage, Brian had decided that, like the grandfather he had never known, he wanted to study medicine.

Brian had a number of reasons for this decision, some clear and obvious, others very private. The clear and obvious ones were that he was interested in people; he saw the effects of chronic illness on his father, and on others, he was good at the relevant subjects at school, and being a doctor was a well-paid and well-respected profession, always in demand in all countries.

Brian's very, very private reasons had to do with certain attractions he felt for people with disabilities, and he knew that being a doctor was likely to bring him into contact with such people. The most obvious example, of course, was his childhood friend, Cathy, with her polio-paralysed leg. But there were others, and Brian was particularly fascinated by people with amputations.

He could never explain why – even to himself – disabled people generally and amputees in particular had a special attraction for him. This started in early childhood, so it predated any sexual attraction. His father had a friend who had been with him in the army during the war, and had lost a leg. He wore a peg-leg, with a lockable hinge at the knee. Brian, at the age of four, was fascinated by the fact that, instead of a foot, what extended from the bottom of this man's right trouser leg was what looked like the shaft of a broomstick, with a rubber tip like the end of a crutch. He remembered afterwards at home getting a stick, tying up his leg and tying the stick to it, and pretending to have a peg-leg like his father's friend.

After this, he always seemed to note and remember when he saw any amputee. He was curious as to what it would be like to lose a leg (he hardly ever saw anyone missing an arm, except for the statue of Nelson on top of the pillar in O'Connell Street in Dublin – which was afterwards blown up by the IRA in 1966). They were probably less disabled than wheelchair-bound paraplegics – certainly less so than quadriplegics, but the fact that they were missing a major part of their body, with either an empty space where it should have been, or an artificial and rather mechanical replacement, fascinated him. However, he kept this fascination very much to himself, never telling anyone else about it.

As he grew, and became more knowledgeable, he realised this was a strange attraction that he had, which he could never have explained to anyone. Later on, when he reached puberty, this fascination became focussed on amputee women, especially pretty ones. The problem was that there were very few pretty amputee women, and he wouldn't have known how to meet them or what to say even if he came across one. And, of course, he didn't want to be labelled a pervert, which he was certain would happen if anyone got to know his predilection. Of course, pretty girls in general had a fascination for him, as for most teenage boys, so it was not just amputees that he focussed upon, but they held a special attraction for him in his fantasies.

By the summer of 1964, Susan and Helen Ryan had developed such a sufficiently close friendship that Susan invited Helen and Lucy to come and stay with her and Brian in County Cork (it was during Brian's summer holidays; he was sixteen and Lucy was nine). They went on various outings – into both Cork City and Waterford, and to Youghal – where they saw Myrtle Grove, the house that Sir

Walter Raleigh had owned, followed by a picnic on Ferry Point, directly across the River Blackwater from Youghal.

At the beginning of April 1965, shortly before the Easter holidays were to commence, Brian was quite badly injured in a rugby match at his school. His left radius and ulna (the bones of the forearm) were broken midway between the elbow and the wrist. He was taken to hospital in Dublin and his arm was x-rayed, revealing quite complex fractures, which necessitated an operation and insertion of a plate and screws to stabilise the fractures. Brian was in hospital over Easter, and when he was discharged his arm was in a cast from his knuckles to above the elbow, supported by a sling.

The doctors in the hospital, speaking to both Brian and his mother, advised that he should not participate further in contact sports, but that when he recovered he could be active in such sports as running, swimming, cycling, tennis, and cricket.

Brian spent most of the summer term in 1965 with his left arm in a cast, unable to participate in any sports. This was the end of the first year of his two-year leaving certificate course. Brian's experiences as a patient confirmed his desire to become a doctor.

In the summer of 1965, when he was out of plaster and the holidays had commenced, Susan took Brian to Paris and then to the Loire Valley on holiday, by way of a treat. They flew from Dublin to Paris, spent four days in the city, and then travelled by train to Orleans, where Susan hired a car. They spent one night in Orleans, Blois, Tours, Angers, Nantes and two nights in Saint Nazaire, before returning by train to Paris and flying back to Dublin.

Brian completed his leaving certificate in the early summer of 1966, with good grades. He applied to various universities, including Trinity in Dublin, Queens in Belfast, and both Oxford and Cambridge. The two latter universities he had applied for a year earlier and received conditional acceptance subject to getting the requisite grades in his leaving certificate, passing their separate entrance examinations, and passing an interview. By the time of leaving school, he had completed all except the interview for Oxford, and had both the entrance exam and interview outstanding for Cambridge. Shelving the latter application, he was accepted for interview at Oxford prior to the start of the Michaelmas term (in October 1966).

That summer, the visit by Helen and Lucy two years previously was reciprocated – Brian and Susan went to stay with them in Sussex for a few days, before all four went on holiday to the Isle of Man. By this stage, Brian, at eighteen, considered himself an adult, a school-leaver, and about to go to university to study medicine. Lucy, at the age of eleven, was just on the verge of puberty. Brian thought of Lucy as still very much a child, albeit a very pretty one. Being something of a connoisseur of music, he did greatly admire her skills in playing the violin.

In due course Brian took and passed his interview for Oxford, and commenced medical school in Balliol College at the Michaelmas term, October 1966. His course consisted of three years' pre-clinical work and three years of clinical work as a junior doctor in the Radcliffe Infirmary.

As Brian studied medicine, he learned that he had been entirely correct to never reveal to anyone his fascination with disabled people, particularly amputees. Medicine did regard it as a psychologically deviant behaviour, and society generally – in circles where it was known – regarded it as a perversion (in much the same way that, at that time, homosexuality was regarded – which was still illegal in England until 1967, and much later in Ireland). There was even a medical name for such a condition – *acrotomophilia*. He was well aware that if his attraction ever became known, he would be debarred from the medical profession, and if he had qualified he would be struck off the register.

This caused him to undertake a great deal of inner soul-searching. On the one hand, he didn't see why he should feel shame or self-loathing for an attraction that was, to all intents and purposes, inherent in him and not something he deliberately chose, like admiring blondes or girls with blue eyes. On the other, he was aware that some people with such tendencies could develop into real perverts – stalking those to whom they were attracted and focussing entirely on the sexualisation of the disability or amputation. Brian was far too much of a gentleman to consider doing such things. He did, briefly, consider trying to get in touch with his childhood friend, Cathy, to see if she had ever carried out her expressed desire to have her paralysed leg amputated, but he quickly put it out of his thoughts.

Brian did have a couple of brief dalliances with girls while at university, but generally his studies were too intense to spend much time socialising, and his time was even more limited when he commenced clinical work.

Holidays from university were mostly spent back in Ireland with his mother, though in the summers of 1969, 1970, and 1971 he did make brief visits to Sussex to see Helen and Lucy. He sympathised with them after Barney's death, and enjoyed listening to Lucy playing her violin. By 1971, when she was sixteen, Brian considered Lucy to have grown into a stunningly beautiful young woman – though of course still rather too young for him to consider, even if he had time to go courting. He did sympathise with her on the issue of being bullied at school, telling her that he had also suffered from this. He agreed that, for her, doing her 'O' and 'A' levels at the technical college or – in the case of music – with private tuition, was probably a good solution.

Once he graduated from medical school and commenced in the Radcliffe Infirmary, Brian began the usual round of rotations in the various departments of the hospital – A & E, paediatrics, oncology, gynaecology, cardiology, general medical and general surgical, orthopaedics, etc.

He was, of course, absolutely stunned when he heard, via his mother, in the autumn of 1972, that Lucy had been in a motorcycle accident, had suffered severe injuries, and had lost a leg. He had recently graduated and was considering whether to become a GP or go on to specialise, possibly in orthopaedic medicine. Then the offer of a temporary post as a resident physician at a hospital in India had been drawn to his attention. Brian had always wanted to return to India, to see if what he vaguely remembered coincided with the truth. He had applied and was awaiting a response when he heard the news about Lucy.

He rushed down to Sussex to see Lucy. He was deeply concerned for her, and upset at what had happened to her – feelings that completely overtook any thoughts of his fascination with amputees. He found her in hospital, coming to terms with what had happened to her in a way that he thought was surprisingly resilient. Then he learned that she was having an affair – indeed living with – a pot-smoking hippy called Zak. Brian was taken aback and quite distressed. He felt that Lucy was far too wonderful a girl, with far too much musical talent, to be caught up in such a scene, and he felt even more concern for her. However, he was far too diplomatic to express his reservations, make his feelings known, or interfere in any way. He went back to Oxford to do some locum work and then heard that his application for the post at a hospital in Bangalore had been successful.

CHAPTER SIX

Before the Crash – Part Three

⊞

Having left school, as agreed between Lucy and her mother, in September 1971, Lucy enrolled at the technical college for 'O' Level courses in maths, English language, English literature, art, geography, history, French, and Spanish, and commenced 'O' Level music theory lessons with her violin and piano teacher. However, because she was essentially a part-time student, she usually had time at home at some point during the day. Often, for practical reasons, she relied on her mother to drive her to college or collect her afterwards (occasionally she would get the bus, but it was mostly the times didn't fit), which sometimes adversely impacted her mother's work patterns. As a result, having by now become slightly more affluent, she bought Lucy a second-hand Honda 50 motorbike for her seventeenth birthday (March 1972), on the understanding that she would get lessons, take her test and get a full bike licence – which in due course she did.

Three of the courses – history, French, and Spanish – were evening classes, the rest during the day. Other participants included a mixture of young people in their late teens and adults ranging from early twenties to one or two in their sixties. One girl that Lucy had been casually friendly with both in primary school and grammar school, Mandy, was also doing the two English courses (she had failed them in school, and was doing resits). Mandy and Lucy naturally gravitated to each other and sat beside each other in classes, and in the canteen.

Mandy had become friendly with three slightly older boys who were doing engineering courses, and a couple of months into the term she introduced them to Lucy as Zak, Davy, and Kevin. At first Lucy found it difficult to tell them apart – they all had long hair and beards, and they used expressions that she was unfamiliar with – "cool", "turned-on", "far out", "freaked out". She learned that, as well as being part-time engineering students, they were members of a rock band that played gigs in some of the local nightclubs, with Zak on vocals and lead guitar, Davy on vocals and bass, and Kevin on drums. Mandy also sometimes joined them as a vocalist. Their band was called *Tangerine Sunset*. When they learned that Lucy played violin and piano, they were keen to have a few sessions with her – indeed they were looking for a keyboard player. Kevin owned a multi-track recorder, and suggested that, as well as maybe playing keyboard, Lucy could record a few violin tracks to layer with the live music.

Mandy thought all this was a great idea, but Lucy was far from keen. Very reluctantly, after Christmas and New Year, she agreed to have a practice session with them. She explained that she normally played from sheet music, and had never really tried 'jam' sessions, or improvisations, though she recognised that many great composers and musicians in the classical genre as well as jazz had frequently engaged in improvisation.

Zak advised that the session would be in his parents' garage, and it transpired that they lived several miles away from Lucy. Zak said he would pick her up in the group's van on the evening that had been arranged for the initial practice session (one of the evenings when she didn't have evening classes).

Accordingly, towards the end of March 1972, not long after Lucy's seventeenth birthday, Zak arrived in a beaten-up old Volkswagen camper, painted with rainbows and flower motifs in psychedelic colours, and Lucy – somewhat reluctantly – climbed in, clutching her violin. Zak and his parents lived in quite a large, very old, detached house on the edge of the county. The house was partly brick and partly half-timbered, with mullioned windows and rooms with old oak beams across the ceilings. The 'garage' was closer to being a barn, filled with an assortment of amps, keyboards, guitars (acoustic and electric), a drum kit, and several battered old settees. There was also a turntable and sound system, with collections of LPs including The Beatles, The Rolling Stones, Bob Dylan, Pink Floyd, Van Morrison, Santana, Cream, Deep Purple, The Incredible String Band and many others. The Beatles' *Lucy In The Sky With Diamonds* was on the turntable, playing, which Lucy took as a good omen – given her name and the fact that it was a track she already knew. Mandy was there, along with Davy and Kevin. On one wall was a poster of what appeared to be a Hindu deity. Some incense sticks, what Zak referred to as joss sticks, were burning in a holder, adding the scent of sandalwood to the air.

"Hey, guys," Davy said. "Let's chill out before we begin." He waved everyone towards one of the settees, and pulled out what to Lucy looked like a tobacco pouch and cigarette paper, and began rolling what seemed to be a large cigarette. They all sprawled onto the settees, and Lucy also sat, in a rather more upright posture, her violin case beside her. Davy lit his large cigarette, and drew heavily on it before passing it to Zak, who took a draw, and held it out to Lucy. The smell of it was sweet and slightly cloying, mixing with the incense.

"I don't smoke," she said.

"No worries," Zak said, "though it isn't just tobacco." He handed the cigarette to Mandy, who took a puff and passed it on to Kevin.

"You'll have a cup of herb tea?" asked Davy, looking at Lucy, but with a slight sideways wink at Zak. Lucy didn't want to seem churlish, so she agreed, and Davy got up and went to the back of the barn, where it transpired there was a kettle, a sink, and a cupboard with mugs and other bits and pieces. He came back with a steaming mug, and handed it to Lucy.

The tea smelt similar to the smoke. Lucy sipped it cautiously. It was palatable, though not quite what she would have wanted, but she proceeded, sipping it slowly while the others enjoyed their smoke, passing the one big 'cigarette' from hand to hand, each taking a long draw. Conversation was desultory, the chief sound being the tracks of The Beatles.

Lucy started to feel relaxed. The atmosphere was peaceful, the music hypnotic. Her mind started to drift. She continued to sip the tea, until it was finished. As the music progressed through the tracks on the album – *Getting Better, Fixing a Hole, She's Leaving Home,* and *Being for the Benefit of Mr Kite!* – it seemed like the garage and everything in it was pulsing, almost dancing, with the sound. Lucy blinked and looked around. Was it her imagination, or had everything become more colourful, more alive? She was glad she had come. She felt that somehow – she didn't understand how – her companions had generated an incredibly euphoric feeling within the space.

The music finished, and Zak picked up his guitar and strummed a few chords, then picked a riff.

"Lucy, can you do something on the keyboard if I give you a chord sequence?" he asked.

Lucy felt she could do anything – get up and float around the room if required.

"Sure," she said.

Zak outlined the chord sequence he wanted, and set up the keyboard. Lucy sat on the stool at the keyboard, and played a chord.

"What time signature and tempo do you want?" she asked.

"I'll play a bit, you listen, and when you're ready, you come in. You'll hear when the chord changes." Zak proceeded to play. After a minute or so, Lucy joined with a sequence of arpeggiated chords on the keyboard.

"Far out!" exclaimed Davy, picking up his bass, and joining in, as did Kevin at the drumkit. Lucy changed from arpeggios to staccato chords played in a syncopated rhythm, then added a few trills and runs. She was enjoying herself. Mandy rose and started to dance, gyrating to the music, but Lucy hardly noticed her. She was lost in the music, which seemed to be coming through her rather than from her.

Some time later – it might have been five minutes or five hours, she couldn't really tell – the music wound down and they all stopped playing.

It was quite late when Zak drove Lucy home. By that time she had played a bit more, including some improvisations on her violin, and had tried a few puffs of another joint (as the big hand-rolled cannabis cigarettes were called), and was totally stoned from both that and the cannabis tea (which is what she afterwards realised it was).

Feeling strangely and totally uninhibited, Lucy said to Zak, "Thank you for this evening. I really enjoyed it. Will we do it again?"

"Yeah," Zak replied. "It was really cool. You're a very pretty and attractive girl, and one amazing musician. That was quite some session we had – you just totally melded with us. We'll do it again, of course."

"Okay."

Lucy's response didn't begin to express the emotions this conversation had for her. Zak had told her that she was pretty and attractive. Of course he could just be being nice and flattering her, but to Lucy he sounded genuine in what he said. Inwardly she was delighted, thrilled, excited and just a tiny bit apprehensive.

This was the start of Lucy's involvement in the band, and of her relationship with Zak. Slowly she came to realise that she had, in effect, been 'spiked' by Davy (given drugs without her knowledge) that first evening, but because she found the effects so pleasant, she accepted it without demur, although deep down she knew it was totally unacceptable – indeed even criminal – behaviour. Thereafter, when rehearsing or doing sessions with the band Lucy often took a few puffs of a joint. She found it gave her a feeling of slight euphoria and mild but very pleasant hallucinations – enhanced colours, and the sense that everything was vibrating or pulsing with a barely perceptible energy. However, although she was increasingly friendly with Zak, and quite liked Kevin (who seemed to be particularly friendly with Mandy), she was always slightly wary of Davy.

Although the band used the so-called garage at Zak's parents' house, he also had a seafront flat in town, where he lived. When Lucy and the band had done a number of sessions in the garage over a few weeks, and got to know each other a bit more, he invited Lucy back there after one session. Normally she wouldn't have gone, but because she was spaced out from the cannabis she had smoked in the garage, she agreed. It was one evening towards the end of May 1972. Once she was ensconced on the settee in Zak's living room, already stoned, she was soon offered a puff from another joint.

Lucy discovered that another effect of getting stoned on cannabis was that she became much less inhibited. Indeed, so much so that all her sexual hang-ups and taboos and her strictly moralistic Catholic schoolgirl upbringing seemed to simply fly out of the window! She and Zak started kissing, something she had never done before with any boy or man. It started off with light, lip-brushing kisses, but quite quickly developed into deep, passionate French kisses. Next thing she knew, she was almost considering unzipping her jeans and removing them, but despite these thoughts, she retained sufficient composure to know that certainly she wasn't ready! However, she was very aware that Zak potentially wanted to go further.

After a while Lucy struggled up, made her excuses, and got Zak to drive her home, which he did without demur. However, she felt very pleasant as they drove, floating on the clichéd cloud nine. She knew that she would come again, and that the next time she might not be quite so restrained. Lucy was still apprehensive and didn't know how it would be for her to lose her virginity.

The next day, in a tea break at college, Lucy met Mandy, and mentioned that she was somewhat attracted to Zak.

"Yeah, well, why not?" said Mandy. "Kevin and I have been together some time now. It would be great if you and Zak got together."

A few days later Zak invited Lucy to his flat again. She went, and they kissed again. She allowed him to put his arms around her, and fondle her breasts. However, when he started to get a bit more intimate, she backed off and told him she wasn't ready. He responded by again telling Lucy she was pretty, she was a great kisser, and that he knew she was only seventeen, and he could wait. Lucy did feel somewhat reassured, but knew that she couldn't keep putting him off, or he really would lose interest. Anyway, she wasn't at all sure that she wanted to put him off again. Part of really wanted to 'go all the way'.

Lucy therefore visited Zak's flat for a third time, going on her motorbike. It was quite late in the evening, and although it was June and getting towards midsummer it was already dusk and a bit misty, so the view from the window was a blue-grey blur with the sea merging with the sky, with lights starting to come on, surrounded by misty halos of light. It was beautiful. Some soft Indian sitar music, probably by Ravi Shankar, was playing on Zak's high-end hi-fi system. Zak rolled a big joint, and they smoked it and let the effects take hold – the mellow feeling, the enhanced visual beauty of the surroundings, and Lucy's remaining inhibitions slipped quietly away. Zak put his arms around her, and again they kissed. This time her hang-ups really had gone.

"This is comfortable," she said, as she snuggled against him. They kissed and cuddled, he stroked her breasts, and then his hand moved down, lifted the hem of her skirt (on this occasion she was wearing a long cotton tie-dyed skirt, one of a few that she had recently acquired to fit into the hippy scene), placed his hand between her thighs and gently rubbed her crotch through the soft cotton fabric of her panties. For a moment Lucy tensed, and almost pulled sharply away, but at the same time it was a pleasant and very intimate feeling, which she had not expected. After a moment she relaxed and sighed with pleasure – and he went on doing it. After a while Zak temporarily disengaged, rolled another joint, and they smoked and cuddled and kissed, he felt her breasts again, and she ran her fingers through his hair. By now, she wanted him. Zak seemed to be increasingly turned on by her kisses, and by fondling her breasts and between her legs. Indeed, Lucy noticed the bulge in his jeans, and in her uninhibited state she first put her hand on it and rubbed him, then unzipped his fly and put her hand inside, to feel him, something she had previously only fantasised about doing with any man.

Almost before Lucy knew it, Zak had unbuttoned her blouse, unhooked her bra, and slipped her skirt and pants down, while she pulled down his jeans and pants. She still wore her glasses. Zak noticed the small gold crucifix that she still wore, despite her virtual abandonment of practising Catholicism anymore (the crucifix was usually covered by her tops).

"Ah, I see you're a Catholic or an Anglo-Catholic. Are you religious, Lucy?"

"No, my granny gave me this when I made my first communion. Yes, I was brought up a Catholic, but I'm not at all religious now. I'm not even sure there is a god."

"Oh yeah, I think God exists, but not in the way religions teach. God is in the beauty of the universe, and in the life-force within each of us, but not in churches and temples. But your crucifix is beautiful, just the same."

Zak undid a small foil package that he had extracted from the pocket of his jeans before he kicked them off, and pulled out a condom, which he quickly unrolled onto himself. He continued with more of the deep French kisses, then nuzzled Lucy's breasts. He then moved down and started to lick and nuzzle her in the most intimate place. It was her first time to have any real sexual encounter with a man, and for her – despite her lingering doubts – it was a revelation. It felt like electric quivers running through her body, and she moaned with pleasure without even realising she was doing so, passion rising. Zak then moved back up and began the French kissing again, smelling of Lucy – quite a musky aroma, but at the same time highly seductive. She grasped him and guided him into her. For a moment there was a quick stab of pain, but then the feeling was wonderful. Lucy wanted to cling to him with everything she had, one arm around his shoulders, the other holding his head with her fingers in his hair, so they were mouth to mouth, and her legs hooked over the back of him, holding him between her legs as he thrust. Again, without any conscious thought of doing so, she moaned, and came to climax, as did Zak.

At last passion was spent, and they relaxed against each other. Lucy pushed her glasses up her nose – they had almost come off during their lovemaking.

"Lucy, you're a wonderful lover," Zak said, softly. "First time?"

"Yeah," she sighed. "It was fabulous. And you're not so bad yourself."

After a while Lucy needed to pee, and asked Zak where the bathroom was. He told her, and she got up, still stark naked (apart from her glasses), and went to the bathroom. She had a quick wash as well as a pee (she didn't want to go home smelling of having just had sex), and returned to the living room. Zak had got dressed, and Lucy quickly followed suit.

Thus, Lucy lost her virginity. She liked Zak; he was reassuring and gentle and sex with him was a wonderful experience. However, she was aware that she wasn't madly in love with him. Lucy didn't know if that would come through time, or, maybe, being madly in love was just a romantic fiction.

About this time, Lucy did her 'O' levels and passed all subjects commendably, getting top marks in music, English, and art, good grades in history, geography, domestic science, and passes in maths, French, biology, and chemistry. She subsequently enrolled in 'A' level classes in the three top subjects, hoping to go to university or music college, possibly to become a music teacher.

A few days after her first experience of having sex, Lucy again visited Zak's flat. After a few joints, sprawled on his old settee, they adjourned to his bedroom (his bed was a double matrass on the floor, with a sheet, a pillow, and an opened-out sleeping bag as a quilt). Lucy took off her jeans (flares, no skirt this time) and this time removed her glasses. They made love again, but somehow, although it was more comfortable on the bed, it wasn't quite so satisfying. Zak initially asked Lucy to go on top, but after trying this, they ended up missionary-style, finding this more comfortable.

Afterwards they chatted for a bit, had a coffee, smoked another joint, and then Zak drove Lucy home, putting her motorbike in the back of his van.

Over the next few weeks Helen expressed strong reservations about Lucy's relationship with Zak, whom she met on a few occasions. She didn't understand what the attraction was in being a hippy, listening to rock music (which she detested), taking drugs (which she regarded as very sinful), being anti-establishment, or – for men – having long hair, and for both sexes wearing such floppy and untidy clothes.

"Be careful, Lucy. I think you're making a big mistake going out with him!" she declared.

Her view of Zak, and her disapproval of Lucy seeing him, led to several very heated arguments and culminated, during the summer holiday period, in Lucy packing her bags and moving in with Zak, the exact opposite of what Helen had wanted.

All the members of the band – including Mandy – smoked cigarettes as well as cannabis. Zak and Davy both smoked about twenty a day, Kevin rather less, and Mandy about ten. Although hesitant, Lucy didn't want to be completely the odd one out, so she also started smoking. The first two or three she found disgusting; they gave her a headache and made her feel sick (she did actually throw up after one). These effects, though, quickly passed. Lucy did limit herself, usually to three and absolutely no more than five cigarettes a day. She was aware that her grandfather had been a heavy smoker and had died of lung cancer, and her father had smoked occasional cigars. Although at the time of her grandfather's death the link between smoking and lung cancer had not been clearly established, it was known by the time Lucy started, and she had no desire to smoke too much because of this. However, she started to really enjoy a cigarette after breakfast, with her coffee, one after lunch, and one just before going to bed.

Zak had a collection of books, on the occult, on Eastern philosophy and religion, and books that were popular with hippy 'seekers of truth', and he suggested to Lucy that she might like to read some of them. Accordingly Lucy read and enjoyed Khalil Gibran's *The Prophet*, and Richard Bach's *Jonathan Livingstone Seagull*, was sceptical about *The Aquarian Gospel*, and even more sceptical about 'Lobsang Rampa's' *The Third Eye*, and could make neither head nor tail of any of the writings of Alice A. Bailey.

Further sessions with the band included several takes in a recording studio (the three guys had been saving for some time to pay for this) – and there was some talk of cutting a record, either a single with a B side, or maybe an album (they recorded a sufficient number of tracks to fill an album), but at the time not much seemed to come of it. As well as playing keyboard, Lucy recorded several violin tracks to be layered into the recordings. The band also did a few live gigs, two at small impromptu outdoor festivals along the south coast, one at the wedding of some hippie friends of Davy's, and several in a few local nightclubs including one in Brighton. These gigs were unpaid except for the nightclubs, from which Lucy got her share of the takings – not a huge amount, but still worthwhile. The band didn't have any ancillary staff, so Davy and Kevin acted as 'roadies' – loading and unloading all the equipment into Zak's old VW van. Kevin had done an electrical course and did most of the setup. The equipment consisted of an amplifier, a mixer, Kevin's multi-track tape deck, several speakers (including monitors), microphones and stands, drum kit, keyboard, both electric and acoustic guitars (including electric bass guitar), and lots of leads. Lucy carried her own violin, but made a point of never taking it with her when she was on her motorbike.

It was after one of the sessions in the garage, in the early autumn of 1972, when Lucy, aged seventeen-and-a-half, quite stoned, was riding her motorbike from the garage at Zak's parents' house to his flat, that the accident happened. She was rounding a right-hand bend at a fair speed, and as she did so a tractor pulled out of a gate in front of her. Lucy braked hard, but lost control completely and hit a stone wall, still at considerable speed, and her left knee (the one she had gashed on the ice nearly thirteen years previously) took the full force of the impact.

CHAPTER SEVEN

Rehabilitation – a New Reality

✠

Before she was discharged from the hospital, Lucy received an unexpected visit from Brian, her 'Aunty' Susan's son, who was now working as a locum doctor in Oxford. He embraced Lucy warmly, asked her about her rehabilitation, and seemed somewhat taken aback when she told her about her relationship with Zak.

As she recovered from the accident, one of the recriminations and areas of contention between Lucy and her mother was regarding insurance. Helen wanted Lucy to claim against the farmer driving the tractor. She thought that, having lost a leg, Lucy should be due tens if not hundreds of thousands of pounds. Lucy's insurance was only third party, fire and theft, and she knew that the insurance company, before making any substantial insurance claims, would seek medical evidence. She had been under the influence of cannabis, a prohibited and illegal substance, had probably been going too fast for the possibility of an unseen vehicle around the bend, and she therefore had no desire to make a claim only to end up not only losing a leg but with a fine or prison sentence and a criminal record as well. Rightly or wrongly, she felt that, as the accident was as much her fault as the farmer's (if not more so), any compensation or insurance payout would be fraud. She had no idea whether the hospital had taken samples from her at the time of her admission, and, if so, whether they had evidence of her being under the influence of cannabis, but she didn't dare to risk it. Nor did she want to admit to her mother that she had been stoned at the time of the accident, but in the end she did so to prevent her mother from pushing too hard for an insurance payout.

Lucy was also somewhat miffed when she realised that her mother had contacted her father in Australia to tell him about the accident. A letter from him arrived addressed to Lucy, full of sympathy and best wishes, apologies that he hadn't been a better father to her, a cheque for one hundred pounds, and an open invitation to come and visit him and his partner in Sydney. Despite her initial annoyance at her mother over this, Lucy quickly realised that her father did have a right to know what had happened, and if he was sorry for the past, so much the better. She had no intention, though, of going to visit him.

Once she was reasonably able to get around on her prosthesis, Lucy moved back in with Zak. Sex with Zak, after her amputation, had initially been something of a hurdle for both of them to face. For a start, Lucy wondered whether Zak or any other man would ever look twice at her, now she had only one leg and a bag on her tummy. She was sure that both her stump, which she considered ugly and unattractive, and her colostomy bag, with its unpleasant noises and the potential for even more unpleasant and disgusting contents (which she was always terrified might leak) would put off nearly any man. Zak had visited her in the hospital many times, and had been reassuring. However, Lucy was very self-conscious, and wasn't sure how Zak would react to seeing her naked with only her short, scarred stump where her left leg had been, not to mention her colostomy bag. She also wasn't sure initially whether she would be able to perform, whether she would find sex as fulfilling, and how it would be to be unable to wrap her legs around Zak as she had previously done. For his part, Zak was scared of hurting Lucy, and therefore quite tentative to begin with in his lovemaking. However, the fears proved groundless. Lucy discovered that, even with only one leg and a bag, she still seemed to be attractive and sexy, and that Zak was not put off.

Of course, if she had her colostomy reversed, the bag would no longer be an issue.

She also discovered a few surprising advantages to her amputation. On one occasion, not long after she had moved back with Zak, when she had quite severe phantom limb pain, she asked him to massage her stump. She quickly discovered that the therapeutic effect of having someone else massage her stump was considerably greater than if she did it herself. She also noticed that Zak not only enjoyed it but seemed to become quite aroused by the process, and it subsequently led to them having sex (despite the lingering phantom pains, which by then had greatly eased). This, more than anything, reassured Lucy that she could still be sexy. They also discovered that some new and very intimate positions became possible.

It was now early spring of 1973, six months since Lucy's accident and amputation. Knowing that her exams were fast approaching, she spent more time studying and less time smoking dope or playing with the band, and – of course – less time having sex with Zak. In due course she passed all three 'A' levels with reasonably good grades (and a very good grade in music, thanks to Mr Scott, her teacher).

By this time, Lucy had come to realise that, although her disability impacted on almost every aspect of her life, she was not only getting used to it, but ceasing to think about it so much. It was becoming just an aspect of her life that she was adjusting to and coped with, now mostly without any great thought or upset. It was, for example, as much second nature to her to reach for her crutches when she got up in the morning as it was for her to put on her glasses. She remembered how she used to be able to run up and down stairs. Now Lucy went up and down stairs one step at a time, real leg first going up, prosthesis first coming down (although coming down she had been shown that, by placing her prosthetic foot so that the heel rested on the edge of each step, with the toe out over it, she could come down step over step). She had quickly got used to it and didn't think too much about it. It was only when she got phantom limb pains, when people very obviously stared at her, or when she found that she couldn't easily do something she had previously taken for granted (such as going up the ladder into the loft in her mother's house to get down the Christmas decorations – easy enough wearing her prosthesis, though slow and cumbersome and very scary, especially coming down, but a major challenge without it), that she felt upset, annoyed or frustrated. Even the discomfort from wearing her prosthesis became relatively normal, and the relief of taking it off was rather like that of taking off a pair of tight and uncomfortable shoes after a long day of wearing them.

Over time, as all swelling in her stump disappeared and the muscles no longer being used shrank, Lucy found that, regardless of the number of stump socks she wore, the socket was loose, and she experienced what the medics referred to as 'pistoning' – that is, her stump would slide up and down inside the socket as she walked, like a piston in a cylinder, which was extremely uncomfortable, tended to make rude noises, and led to bruises and abrasions. This resulted in her having to return to the limb-fitting centre to be re-cast for a new socket. She learned that this was quite normal, and some amputees would need two, three, or even four new sockets before a reasonably long-term fit was achieved.

Lucy's surgeons also decided, at this stage, that her colostomy could be reversed, so she went back into hospital for this surgery. Afterwards she once again found herself initially in intensive care, with IV, nasogastric tube, and urinary catheter. However, her recovery was relatively quick. She was in hospital for just under two weeks, and was greatly relieved to be discharged without a stoma or a colostomy bag, despite the pain and discomfort of the surgery, or the by now unusual sensation of having to poo again in the normal way. The scars on her abdomen had increased, but she no longer cared about that.

It was one day in Zak's flat that she discovered an unexpected, and rather unconventional purpose for her prosthesis. The foam cover, designed to make the artificial limb look something like a leg, seemed to cry out for a different kind of filling, a different kind of solace. The idea, impulsive and rebellious, sparked within her as a mischievous whisper: a secret stash. She got a knife and hollowed out some of the foam. Her small personal supply of cannabis (which Zak had given her), carefully stored within the hollow of the foam was now shielded from prying eyes and unexpected searches. It was a secret hidden in plain sight, a bold, defiant act in the face of her own limitations. The prosthesis, originally a symbol of her vulnerability, had become a clandestine repository, a testament to her enduring spirit of rebellion.

She'd found a strange comfort in this secret, a small rebellion in the face of adversity. It was a defiant act, a reclaiming of control, a little piece of her old life nestled within the new, altered reality she inhabited. The cannabis, once a symbol of carefree freedom, became a source of quiet solace, easing the emotional pain that still lingered, a bitter aftertaste of the crash.

Another thing Lucy did to regain a bit of self-esteem was to go to her dentist and ask about having her teeth straightened. They had never been badly misaligned, but Lucy had always been slightly self-conscious of them, and although this now seemed a very small thing in comparison with her amputation, she wanted at least her smile to be as attractive as possible. Accordingly, she was, in due course, fitted with orthodontic braces on both her top and bottom teeth – double rows of what seemed like railway tracks to her! However, she knew this to be a temporary measure, although one that would probably last at least a year, maybe eighteen months, with appointments every three months to adjust the braces as they pulled her teeth into line. Zak exclaimed when he saw her, but didn't dislike the effect, though Lucy insisted he be very careful when kissing her as she thought he might cut his tongue on her braces.

Life in Zak's flat and sessions with the band provided a necessary distraction, though the shadows of the accident still haunted her. The other members of the band, and a number of other 'drop-outs', would frequent the flat, often staying overnight, treating it as a communal crash-pad. This communal living, while not always harmonious, offered Lucy a sense of belonging, a network of support that helped her navigate the challenges of her new life. Her friends, a kaleidoscope of personalities united by their shared embrace of alternative lifestyles, welcomed her back with open arms, their acceptance a balm to her wounded spirit. Their free-spirited nature, their willingness to defy convention, helped her to redefine her own identity, to see herself not as a victim but as a survivor, albeit one with a prosthetic leg and a secret hidden within its foam.

However, when out on her own, Lucy became aware of other aspects of her disability that she had not imagined. She found that if, for any reason, she went out on crutches – and especially if she went out on crutches wearing either a skirt that was not at least ankle-length or jeans with the empty leg folded up and pinned, not only did people stare (which she was getting used to) but some – nearly always men – started following her. One evening, when she had been crutching along the seafront after dinner, and sat on a bench to smoke a cigarette, a young man – rather drunk – came and sat beside her.

"Hello, darlin'. I've been watching you," he said. "You're ever so sexy on them crutches. I bet your stump is a real turn-on. Care to give me a peek?"

Lucy, completely shocked, told him to get lost. She was prepared, if the worst came to the worst, to use her crutches as weapons to defend herself, but eventually he wandered away. Lucy didn't want to be followed back to Zak's flat, so to make sure, she went into a shop and spent some time pretending to be looking at various things, before buying a packet of cigarettes and exiting, carefully checking that he was nowhere to be seen.

Thus, Lucy became aware of those men who, attracted to amputees, were not above becoming stalkers and predators. Although she never mentioned the incident to anyone, she was extra vigilant after this – especially if she went out on crutches without her prosthesis.

Nevertheless, she experienced a certain joy in moving on her crutches, which she didn't on her prosthesis. Although the effort required was substantially more than simply walking had been before her accident, she found she was able to move very quickly and fluidly on them, and it gave her a slight high feeling (without need for cannabis!), something similar to what she had previously felt running.

Lucy liked Zak, but she wasn't madly in love with him and she sensed that, though he thought she was pretty, enjoyed sex with her, and liked her as a person, he wasn't madly in love with her either. They made no demands of each other, and asked for no commitments. She knew he had had other women, but she never asked him about them and he never volunteered any information.

Zak did invite Lucy to participate in an acid trip with him. He arranged this towards the end of June 1973 (close to the summer solstice), starting before dawn (so effectively the middle of the night). Lucy decided to go on her crutches, wearing warm clothes in the chilly pre-dawn air, and she and Zak got into his battered old VW van. He was wearing a rather shabby Afghan goatskin coat, with the hair on the inside. He had with him a small battery-operated ghetto blaster, a bag of cassette tapes (which were just starting to become popular around that time), and a bag with food and drink. They parked near a country railway station, then walked under an archway of the railway line, beside a golf course, and across a field to the edge of a wood. It was just starting to get light in the eastern sky. Zak turned left along a path, and Lucy swung along beside him on her crutches. They went as far as a knoll at the edge of the wood, looking down across the fields, and sat on the remains of an old stone wall. Zak gave Lucy a small square of what looked like pink blotting paper.

"Suck it, chew it, swallow it whole – doesn't really matter," he said. He took another 'tab' himself, and fiddled with the ghetto blaster and the cassettes. A succession of tracks played – quite softly – as they watched the sun come up and the LSD started to take effect. Tracks included Cat Stevens singing *Morning has Broken*, The Beatles – *Strawberry Fields Forever* and *Lucy in the Sky with Diamonds* (which Zak dedicated to Lucy!) and Wagner's *Siegfried Idyll*, as well as some of their own tracks from the recording sessions they had done.

Lucy had never seen a sunrise like that one. The colours seemed so incredibly intense and beautiful, colours she had never seen before and could never have imagined, and she was part of it and it was part of her. Lucy suddenly knew that, if she wanted to, she could fly! She told Zak this, and he calmly said, "Yeah, it's great, but don't try it!"

He helped to guide her through a very intense but fantastically beautiful experience, where the trees seemed to be wise, sentient beings watching over them, and as she breathed, Lucy was convinced that the wind from her breath rustled the leaves. Indeed, everything was connected to her, and she was part of everything. She understood what Zak meant about God being in the beauty of the universe and in the life-force within her. As Zak played more tracks on the ghetto blaster, it seemed as though the whole universe danced to the music – or perhaps the universe was already dancing and the music spontaneously sprang into being as a result!

Several hours passed (although Lucy was not conscious of time) in this euphoric state, and then gradually everything returned to normality. Zak had brought juice and sandwiches, and they had a picnic lunch, before getting up and making their way back to where his van was parked.

About three or four weeks after her first acid trip, Lucy took a second, in Zak's flat. It started off nicely, with heightened and shimmering colours, and solid objects seeming to become insubstantial and gossamer light. But then a poster on the wall of the Hindu god Kali turned into a demon that came to life, its eyes watching her, filled with hatred. She was transfixed with terror. When she looked away, she found another even more terrifying demon looking at her from another poster. Lucy spent the last hour or two of the trip almost screaming in terror, knowing that she had gone mad, and that this was Hell. Zak tried to pull her out of it, and if it hadn't been for his efforts, she would probably have taken a kitchen knife and slashed her throat or stabbed herself.

She was a quivering wreck by the time normality was back and knew it had all been a hallucination. But she wanted no more acid trips. In the first one she had seen Heaven, but in the second she had also seen Hell, and it was an experience she had no wish ever to repeat. Lucy knew that, for her, continuing to mess with such drugs would lead to bad consequences – scrambled brains, psychiatric illness, maybe even something like heroin addiction – if she survived! It was enough for her to survive as an amputee without adding severe psychiatric illness to her condition.

In regard to heroin addiction, it was just after this that Lucy discovered that Zak didn't just smoke cannabis and take occasional LSD trips. She had a small supply of prescription codeine tablets for her post-accident need for stronger than over-the-counter painkillers. She knew these were highly addictive, and was strict with herself to only take when real necessity arose. One day, when she was in considerable pain (there was an area of her stump that was especially sensitive, and pressure on it tended to trigger bad phantom limb pains), she discovered that these had vanished. She asked Zak if he knew what had happened to them. Somewhat shame-facedly he told her he had taken them.

"They're an opiate, and my supply has run out until I score more next week," he said.

"I didn't know you were into opiates!"

"Yeah, well... I like to smoke something a bit stronger than hash sometimes. And it does my head in when I can't get it – or a substitute like your tablets. Sorry I took them, Lucy. Can you say they accidentally got flushed down the toilet, or something?"

When Lucy got a fresh supply of codeine she made sure to put it in the secret compartment in her prosthesis, which Zak was unaware of. She kept a closer eye on Zak, concerned both at his dishonesty and for his welfare if he was into harder and more addictive drugs. She came to realise that, although his parents (with whom he seemed to have a rather strained relationship) were extremely well off, and – despite their differences – provided him with quite a generous allowance, and that he had a part-time job as a mechanic, most of his money went on buying drugs; scoring, as he termed it. While cannabis and LSD were relatively cheap, heroin – which he liked to smoke – was not. Although she was not deeply in love with him, Lucy was sufficiently attached to Zak that she was seriously worried by the increasing periods when he would be completely out of it, in a heroin trance. She was also concerned at finding his paraphernalia – burnt out candles and sticky foil 'pipes' – lying around. In the circles she now frequented she had heard the term 'chasing the dragon', and instinctively knew this was what Zak was doing, and that it was a road to inevitable self-destruction.

CHAPTER EIGHT

The Trip is Planned

�֍

By this stage, in the summer of 1973, Lucy had put on hold her plans to go to university or music college. For some time Zak, the other members of the band and Davy's girlfriend, Jessica, had been talking of going to India. Now Zak wanted Lucy to join them. The plans for the trip gradually coalesced into a whirlwind of excitement and anticipation that momentarily eclipsed everything else, including Lucy's lingering pain and her plans for university. Zak's vintage VW camper, a symbol of freedom and adventure, was being meticulously prepared, a testament to the group's unwavering optimism. Their collective dreams of a spiritual awakening, a journey of self-discovery, coupled with expectations of unlimited supplies of hash and opium, fuelled their preparations, temporarily obscuring the stark reality of the financial constraints they faced.

Funding the trip was a big issue. Zak and Davy had part-time jobs as mechanics, and had set aside a certain amount. Kevin did various electrical jobs for people, for cash payments, part of which he also contributed. Jessica worked in a wholefoods shop and as well as money, provided dried beans, lentils, brown rice, olive oil and any other non-perishable foodstuffs she thought would be useful. Mandy did a few stints as a shop assistant, and contributed from her wages. However, for the five of them, the attitude was one of not really caring whether they had money or not – somehow they would get by. For Lucy, while she would have liked to take a similar devil-may-care attitude, the reality for her, as an amputee, of undertaking a long, gruelling journey through countries where healthcare standards were more rudimentary, was of greater importance, and she knew she had to be slightly more responsible. Lucy had saved most of her share of payments from the nightclub gigs the band had done, plus some of her father's hundred pounds, and she provided her share of the funds from this. One of the preparations was to convert most of their currency to travellers' cheques, as at that time there was a limit of fifty pounds per person in British currency that each traveller could take out of the country.

For Lucy, the trip, a symbol of escape, promised not only a chance to experience several different cultures but also an opportunity to distance herself from the painful memories that still haunted her, without fear of running into people she had known before her accident. These were people who inevitably looked aghast (especially if she was on crutches instead of her prosthesis), and said, "Oh my god, Lucy! Whatever happened?"

She hated it when this happened, and she had to retell the story of what was an extremely traumatic event. She hated even more the sympathy, verging on pity, that this generated. She longed to go somewhere where no-one knew her, aside from Zak and her other friends who were planning on going on the trip, and no questions about her accident need arise.

She had been an amputee for almost a year now. Her prosthetic leg, once a symbol of her injury and a reminder of her vulnerability, had become an unexpected tool, a silent accomplice in her new life. The foam cover had been repurposed as a clandestine hiding place for her cannabis stash, along with her painkillers, a secret compartment that provided a sense of control in a world that often felt chaotic and unpredictable. The stash itself was a small, comforting rebellion against the norms of society. It wasn't just about getting high; it was about asserting her independence, a small act of defiance against a set of circumstances that had taken so much from her.

It was amidst the flurry of packing and preparations that the opium-smuggling proposition was first mooted, subtly at first, then with an increasingly insistent push. The offer, initially tempting for its potential to replace the funds expended on their trip, gradually transformed into a far weightier decision. For Lucy it was more than just money; it was a test of her commitment to the group's unorthodox ways, a test of her loyalty to her friends and the intoxicating world of self-expression that she had once embraced wholeheartedly.

Lucy hesitated at first, the memory of the accident still fresh and vivid. Her initial resistance stemmed from a growing awareness that this escapade was pushing the boundaries of acceptable risk. The notion of transporting cannabis – a risky venture in itself – was a transgression she was able to rationalise, but smuggling harder drugs was another matter entirely.

The weight of potential consequences loomed large, a chilling contrast to the idyllic vision of self-discovery that fuelled the trip. However, the persistent encouragement of her friends, especially Davy, their promises of financial security, and the pervasive influence of the intoxicating, rebellious energy of the group gradually eroded her resistance. The desire to escape the haunting memories of the accident, the allure of adventure, the pressure to belong, all played their part in her decision. What also swayed her was that there seemed to be no hard and fast or fixed plan, so she hoped – perhaps wishful thinking on her part – that nothing would come of this, or that if something did materialise, it need not directly involve her.

The preparations for the journey were a whirlwind of activity, a chaotic ballet of packing, last-minute errands, and farewells. The van was transformed into a mobile home, filled with clothes, blankets, camping gear, and a hidden compartment within the camper shell, which would, it was supposed, bear witness to the illegal transport of cannabis and heroin, or at least opium to be refined into heroin. The atmosphere was electric, a palpable mixture of excitement and nerves. They meticulously checked every detail, ensuring that their illicit cargo, when obtained, could be secured. Lucy double-checked her own hidden compartment in her prosthetic leg, a quiet, private moment amidst the collective excitement. The small, carefully wrapped packages of cannabis and her requisite painkillers seemed to represent a different kind of freedom, an ironic rebellion hidden within the constraints of her artificial limb. The finality of their preparations created a sense of irrevocable commitment, a step across the threshold into a world where the consequences were yet unknown.

A big question for Lucy was whether to take her violin on the journey. In the end she decided to leave it. It was too precious to risk. Instead, she saved up and bought herself a relatively cheap one to bring with her. It didn't have the sweetness and mellowness of tone, but it did allow her to maintain her skills, even if practice on it was to be somewhat curtailed by the journey. Her good violin she left in the care of her mother.

There were, of course, many practicalities to be gone through before the journey could commence. Lucy had to obtain a new passport, and being an Irish citizen, this involved going to the Irish embassy in London. They all had to get vaccinations – cholera and smallpox, and Lucy went to one of the new family planning clinics and got a supply of contraceptive pills. She also replenished her supply of codeine, stump socks, and stocked up on bandages and first-aid supplies. She went to her optician, had her eyes tested, and got new glasses (two pairs, one as spare), very slightly stronger than her previous ones (minus 5.25 right and minus 5.5 left). These were big round glasses, one with dark metal frames, the other with black plastic frames, which she thought went better with her auburn hair than her previous tortoiseshell frames. She also got herself some clip-on sunglasses. A further appointment for Lucy was with her dentist, to have her braces adjusted. She told the dentist that she would be going away, in all probability for at least three months, maybe four or five, and he said that would be okay so long as she made an appointment to see him as soon as she returned.

Helen Ryan was very apprehensive at the idea of Lucy heading off to India with a bunch of 'long-haired layabouts'.

"You're still rehabilitating from your accident!" she exclaimed. "Whatever do you want to risk your health and your life for, heading off overland to India?"

Lucy tried to explain. "This journey *is* part of my rehabilitation, Mum. I need freedom, and I need to be able to show myself that I can do this."

Reluctantly, Helen accepted that she could not stop Lucy, who was eighteen and legally an adult, free to do as she chose. She gave Lucy two hundred pounds towards the journey (quite a sizeable sum in 1973). This enabled Lucy to put a bit more into the communal pot, and to get some more travellers' cheques.

"By the way, I heard from Susan. As you know, Brian got his qualifications as a doctor, and early last spring he accepted an offer to work in a hospital in India for a year. He was born there, and he said he always wanted to go back. I think he'll still be there for another three or four months. You might look him up."

Lucy said nothing, knowing that India was a vast country with hundreds of millions of people and the chances of her running into Brian was next to zero. Nevertheless, she accepted the card with Brian's contact details, care of a hospital in Bangalore. Privately, she wondered if her mother was thinking that, by the time she got to India, Lucy might need the services of a doctor, preferably a European one.

There was packing to be done, which, in Lucy's case, included a substantial supply of cotton stump socks or liners for her prosthesis.

Her stump had shrunk over time (she no longer had to swathe it in elastic bandages), and although she had been refitted with a new socket (having made sure that her prosthesis did not contain anything illegal prior to and during this process), any changes in her stump due to heat, her monthly cycle, or whether she either gained or lost any weight, had to be compensated for by increasing or decreasing the number of socks, ensuring sufficient padding for a tight fit. She also included her aluminium forearm crutches. While she had grown accustomed to getting around on her prosthesis, it was always a relief to take it off, and there were times when sores and blisters made it sheer hell to wear. At such times, whenever possible, she reverted to crutches, and indeed at home generally she often took off the leg, preferring to use her crutches, finding greater comfort on them. Indeed, if it hadn't been for the possibility of running into someone she had known before her accident, or being accosted or followed by some man with a predilection for amputee women, she would have much preferred to swing along on her crutches most of the time, except when she needed to carry things. Her own self-image had adjusted to accepting herself as one-legged, so apart from encounters with those two categories of people, she no longer felt the need to appear two-legged.

The departure was an emotional crescendo, a mix of tears, laughter, and hopeful goodbyes. The old VW van, lumbering down the road, was more than just a vehicle; it was a symbol of their shared dreams and anxieties, a floating vessel carrying their hopes for self-discovery, and the unspoken weight of their illegal undertaking. As the urban sprawl gave way to the open countryside of Sussex and Kent, and the vistas afforded by the South Downs, the adventure truly began, a journey that would irrevocably alter the course of Lucy's life.

The road ahead stretched before them, promising both untold adventure and the potential for profound danger.

CHAPTER NINE

The Journey Begins – Europe

❖

The van, now affectionately nicknamed 'Gypsy Rose', rattled and groaned its way across the English countryside, a soundtrack to Lucy's burgeoning unease. The initial exhilaration of departure had begun to fade, replaced by a gnawing anxiety that mirrored the persistent thump-thump-thump of the aging engine. She glanced at her companions, a motley crew of free spirits united by their shared rebellion and a thirst for something more than the mundane reality they'd left behind. There was Zak, her boyfriend, who had brought the band together, with his perpetually tangled beard and eyes that held a faraway look; Davy, a wisecracking humourist, with long dark hair and beard, who nevertheless had an 'edge' to him; Kevin, a quiet observer, his gaze often fixed on the road ahead, with a shaggy mop of brown hair; Mandy, Lucy's longtime schoolfriend, but whom she had really only got to know more recently as part of the band, a devil-may-care girl, kind but sometimes thoughtless, with long, straight, dark blonde hair; and Jessica, a redhaired whirlwind of energy and brightly coloured clothing, whose laughter was as infectious as her enthusiasm. The three men took turns doing the driving.

They drove to Dover, and joined the queue for the ferry to Calais, reminding Lucy of her school trip to France in what now seemed like another life. The saloons on the ferry were crowded, the atmosphere stuffy, and the crossing was rough. Lucy, feeling rather seasick, made her way out on deck, grimly holding handrails to keep her balance. On her prosthetic leg, standing and walking on a ship in a rough sea was a whole new ballgame, and several times she almost stumbled and fell. On deck, she clung to the rail, the wind whipping her hair and causing her to pull the duffle coat she was wearing more tightly around herself. Salt spray, blowing in sheets across the open deck, encrusted on her glasses and quickly obscured her vision. She was thankful when the calmer waters at the entrance to the harbour at Calais were reached; she could clean her glasses with a wet tissue, and she and the others could stumble down to the car deck and into their van.

From Calais they set off following the coast in a northeasterly direction, passing through the village of Gravelines before skirting Dunkirk, where thirty-three years earlier the British Army had been evacuated by the 'little ships', under the onslaught of Hitler's forces. From Dunkirk they proceeded into Belgium and turned inland. The countryside was flat, consisting of large fields of grass or of vegetable crops, bounded by canals or lines of trees – mostly poplars. After a bit Lucy, having taken off her leg to be more comfortable, closed her eyes and dozed.

Later, Lucy wasn't sure how much later, they arrived at a campsite, where a number of other travellers – many of them hippies – were also preparing to spend the night. Jessica unpacked a camping stove, brown rice, beans (soaked overnight the previous night, before their departure), and some spinach garnered from a field they had passed on the way, and set about making an evening meal – filling and satisfying, if somewhat bland and tasteless.

Later on, a campfire was lit and travellers from several of the vehicles onsite gathered to sit around it. Several guitars and a harmonica were produced, and songs were sung, joints were rolled and passed around, and philosophical debates were held. Although most of the travellers were British, there were also a few Americans, and one or two Germans and Dutch. Despite her misgivings, Lucy enjoyed the evening, before eventually tucking herself into a sleeping bag, between Jessica and Mandy in the back of the van, which now smelled of a mixture of patchouli oil and cannabis smoke. The men had erected a small tent, which they shared.

The next morning meant washing in cold water at the campsite's facilities, followed by a breakfast of granola, fruit and coffee, and Lucy's post-breakfast cigarette, before continuing their journey.

This was the start of many similar days that passed. They crossed into Germany, skirted around Munich, and proceeded into Austria. The scenery changed – now they had passed through the Black Forest and were skirting the northern edges of the Alps. Lucy gradually got used to sleeping in a sleeping bag in the van, washing in cold water (her stump was particularly sensitive to this), and the general discomforts of travel in a vehicle with five other people and everything they needed for several months. Washing clothes was the most problematic issue. When they could, they used launderettes in the towns they passed through, but such facilities were few and far between, and sometimes they had to resort to hand washing clothes in cold water and hanging them on trees and bushes at camping places. The van smelled of damp laundry, and getting clothes dry – especially when the weather was not conducive, was an ongoing issue.

They stopped for a couple of days in Salzburg. Lucy had seen The Sound of Music as a teenager, and, as a musician, was also aware that the city was where Mozart had been born and lived until he moved to Vienna. As a group they visited the Mirabell Palace Gardens, the Fortress, and the ornate baroque cathedral. Lucy stayed behind in the cathedral. Although she had abandoned her Catholic observance and belief, she stayed for mass and was deeply moved by the ambience of the place, despite her lack of faith. She also visited the museum that now occupied the house where Mozart had been born.

After Salzburg, they headed via Graz into Yugoslavia. Skirting Zagreb, they headed towards Belgrade, stopping in a field at the roadside overnight. Heading on the next day, without further delay, they crossed into Bulgaria and then into Greece, stopping at a campsite in Kavala on the coast of the Aegean Sea, where they spent a couple of days enjoying the sunshine and the sea. Lucy summoned up her courage and, in bra and cut-off jeans (she didn't have a swimming costume), hopped into the water and swam. She loved it – the water supported her and there was a freedom of movement, without prosthesis or crutches, which she had not experienced since her accident. The only downsides were that she had to do it without her glasses, so she couldn't see anything clearly, and her cut-off jeans took ages to dry out afterwards, even in the warm Mediterranean sunshine.

One issue had confounded Lucy when she first encountered it. In an increasing number of places, as they travelled eastward, the public toilets didn't have toilet bowls with seats, just a hole with two raised footplates on either side, where one simply squatted. Lucy, of course, could not squat. It was impossible to balance in the right position on one leg, and the knee hinge of her prosthesis only flexed to 90 degrees, enough to sit but not to squat. Extremely embarrassed, Lucy had to ask Jessica or Mandy to help her, holding her and supporting her as she squatted. She was terrified that, if they let their grip on her slip, she would fall over the hole, which was invariably in a pretty nasty state of uncleanliness. She also swallowed her pride and admitted the problem to Zak. At the next town they stopped in, he went scouting around and found an old wooden crate of the right dimensions (approximately a half-metre cube), which had an open top; he turned it over and with a sawblade on his penknife, cut a six-inch diameter circular hole in what had been the bottom. After this, Lucy was able to place this over any toilet hole and sit as normal.

From Kavala they drove into Turkey, and to Istanbul, a city that seemed to span millennia. The ancient walls whispered stories of empires long gone, while the modern city throbbed with a vibrant energy. It was by far the most exotic place Lucy had yet been to, with its domed mosques and soaring minarets, some of the men wearing fezzes and some of the women hijabs, and the cries of the muezzins calling the faithful to prayer. It seemed to Lucy the epitome of the sights and sounds of the East.

They made their way into the oldest part of the city – Sultanahmet – where both the Hagia Sofia and the Blue Mosque stood, as well as the Topkapi Palace of the Ottoman Sultans until the mid-nineteenth century. The Hagia Sofia was, of course, originally a Christian cathedral – the seat of the Byzantine branch of the Church (which became Orthodox Christianity) – with the largest dome in the world at the time it was built. Later, under the Ottomans, when the city changed from Constantinople (originally Byzantium) to Istanbul, the building became, for a time, a museum and historical site, and then a mosque. Nearly all the mosques in Istanbul – and indeed throughout much of Turkey – drew architectural inspiration from the Hagia Sofia, combining it with superlative Islamic decoration as exemplified by the nearby Blue Mosque.

Across the street from the Blue Mosque was a café, and although it had a Turkish name it also proclaimed itself in English as 'The Pudding Shop', and it was a meeting place for hippies going to and returning from India. Inside was a large message board where people left notes for friends and acquaintances to pick up when they passed through. The café extended into an adjacent garden, and there they relaxed over a meal (Lucy tried hummus and falafels with flatbreads for the first time), drank Turkish coffee or sweetened Turkish tea in little glasses, smoked – both cigarettes and hash, played music, and mingled with others doing the same.

Later they visited both the Blue Mosque and the Hagia Sofia. Although the latter was bigger, older, and still retained some Christian icons and symbols high up on the walls, Lucy found the former the more strikingly beautiful. They had to take their shoes off before entering both mosques, and Lucy was glad that she had put on a pair of socks, so her prosthetic foot was not so obvious. Although very different to Christian cathedrals, there was a similar atmosphere of tranquillity, reverence and spirituality. The space inside the mosques was mostly open, carpeted, brightly lit by huge circular chandeliers as well as fabulous stained-glass windows filled with Islamic designs and quotations from the Quran in flowing Arabic script, with the fabulously decorated dome rising above.

They stayed for some days in Istanbul, and Lucy sent a postcard to her mother (as she subsequently did from several other places along the journey). The Grand Bazaar was a fascinating place to explore, and Davy bought himself a water pipe, which he termed his hubble-bubble, and in which he smoked some very strong hash he had acquired. The rest of them tried a few puffs too.

'Gypsy Rose' – the old VW camper van – needed some mechanical work done before they proceeded. Zak, who owned the van, being a mechanic, did most of the work, assisted by Davy, though at times both of them disappeared, separately, and Lucy was unaware of where either had gone.

The stay in Istanbul gave them all a chance to get all their laundry properly washed and dried. Once the van was sound to continue, they proceeded to get the ferry across the Bosphorus to the Asian side. At that time, a bridge was in the process of being built across the Bosphorus, but it was not yet open. The ferry departed from close to the Galata Bridge across the Golden Horn, an inlet from the Bosphorus, on the European side. The Galata Bridge then, as now, was lined with people fishing. The ferry journey was quite short – half an hour and they were over and driving through the suburbs of Istanbul on the Asian side.

CHAPTER TEN

The Journey Continues – Asia

From eastern Istanbul the van traversed the agricultural hinterland, slowly ascending to the Anatolian Plateau. There the landscape became arid – vast brown and grey stony vistas of patchy dry grass and scrub, with occasional hills and mountains in the distance. En route they skirted around Ankara. It was hot in the daytime, but bitterly cold as night fell, so they pulled in to the side of the road, cooked a hot meal, and then all six of them got into their sleeping bags and huddled together inside the van for warmth.

The next day they continued east, the landscape becoming ever more rugged and remote. The boys had heard that Cappadocia was worth visiting, so they headed for it, and the town of Göreme. The landscape in this area was truly astonishing, something Lucy felt had come straight out of a fairy story. Indeed, one of the features was numerous 'fairy chimneys', strange rock pinnacles that stuck up all over the landscape in weird shapes, some like mushrooms, others like rockets or missiles, and still others like phalluses. Jessica had a camera and took photos, and Lucy did some sketches.

Then they drove on, crossing the flat expanse of the Muş Plain, at last reaching the shores of Lake Van, a vast saline lake in Eastern Turkey at an altitude of more than 5,000 feet. More or less following the shoreline, they arrived in the city of Van, where they spent the night. The next day they pushed on, through rugged but arid mountains, to the border into Iran, at that time still an open, albeit corrupt country ruled over by the Shah. Once through the border formalities they continued to Tabriz, where they stayed overnight before heading to Teheran, where they stayed in a cheap hotel.

During much of the journey the three boys, Zak, Davy, and Kevin, as well as regularly smoking hash, were also not averse to taking 'speed' – amphetamines – to enable them to stay awake and alert enough to drive through unknown, difficult and sometimes dangerous places. Lucy watched silently, with apprehension, and a little knot of worry often formed in the pit of her stomach. The other two girls seemed oblivious to any tension, though this might just have been a show of bravado.

For Lucy, days bled into each other, a blur of dusty landscapes, hot days and bitterly cold nights, and uncomfortable silences. The vibrant beauty of the countryside failed to penetrate the growing darkness within her. The once-exciting novelty of foreign lands and cultures felt muted, dulled by the constant weight of her apprehension. Even amongst the other members of the group, the laughter and carefree spirit of the initial journey were long gone, replaced by a palpable tension that hung heavy in the air, an unspoken understanding that they were all teetering on the brink of potential disaster.

There was the unspoken plan to acquire either heroin or at least unrefined opium as well as cannabis to smuggle back to England on the return journey, to recoup the costs. There was also Zak's heroin addiction, of which they were all aware, but said nothing. Although he was nominally the group leader, and he was primarily the reason Lucy had come on the journey, there were several times when Davy and Kevin effectively had to take over making decisions, looking after the van, and planning the route. After some time, Lucy became aware that Zak was no longer 'smoking' his heroin (heating it in a foil 'pipe' over a candle flame and inhaling the vapour), but had acquired syringes and needles, and was now injecting himself with it. Lucy, who had endured enough injections for legitimate medical reasons to last a lifetime, was horrified, but knew she could not remonstrate with Zak, and so said nothing.

Throughout the journey so far, sex between Lucy and Zak had been confined to those occasions when they stayed in hotels overnight, and not always then. Now, as it progressed, sex became less and less frequent, largely because Zak was either so tired from his stints driving or because he was completely zonked out by his addiction.

Lucy noticed Davy watching her several times, looking speculatively. She didn't altogether trust him. On the surface he was a fun guy, cracking jokes and being good humoured, but there was also a steeliness about him and a sort of grim determination that he mostly kept hidden. Lucy couldn't put her finger on it, but she was wary of him.

From Teheran they headed to Mashad, again intending to stay overnight in a campsite. Here, as they travelled, the heat became oppressive, dust hung in the air, and the van acquired an un-asked-for payload of sandflies with vicious bites. By the time they arrived in Mashad, both Lucy and Kevin became sick with suspected dysentery – vomiting and diarrhoea – and so the group was unable to continue. They checked into a hotel, and Zak, for once resuming his leadership, sought the services of a local doctor for the two sick casualties. An uncomfortable two days passed before they were well enough to continue, feeling weak and rather groggy, and even then they had to wait for visas to get into Afghanistan due to local officialdom. Travellers' cheques had to be cashed and US dollars acquired and passed on as baksheesh before this difficulty was resolved.

At the border, further money had to be exchanged, and they had to get clearance from a doctor before being admitted. The doctor didn't take much interest in them apart from collecting a few dollars, until he saw Lucy, looking wan from being sick, and limping heavily as, having been unable to eat and becoming dehydrated during the illness, she had lost weight. Despite this weight loss, Lucy's stump had swollen in the heat, her socket felt incredibly tight, the stump hurt almost unbearably, her back ached, and the Silesian belt around her waist felt like a corset of fire. Her phantom limb pains, which had been easing off over several months, were also back with a vengeance. The doctor tutted, and took pity on her, issuing a supply of morphine (the opium from which this was derived was, of course, for what Afghanistan was famous). Lucy surreptitiously put this into the secret compartment in her prosthesis – she didn't want Zak to get hold of it, though she knew he would find it easy enough to come by unlimited supplies himself.

Seeing Zak's addiction slowly destroying him made her more determined than ever to avoid addiction herself, so she gritted her teeth and put up with the pain unless it became virtually unbearable. She now only put on her prosthesis when she knew they were making a stop and she would have to get out of the van, and often not even then, preferring to use her crutches. Wearing the leg in the heat and in conditions where washing and skincare were at best not easy, and often impossible, was causing the skin on parts of her stump to break down into suppurating sores. She tried to patch these up as best she could with gauze pads, adhesive dressings and bandages from their first-aid kit, which was rapidly being depleted. Her prosthesis also smelled increasingly strongly, and there was little Lucy could do to counteract this, except covering it with a plastic bin bag to contain the stench. Her supply of clean stump socks was also severely depleted. Proper laundry facilities were scarce, and several of the socks had encrusted stains from her sores that needed more than just a quick rub in cold water with a bar of soap to get rid of them. She was also concerned that one area of her stump, close to the scar, was becoming increasingly painful and sensitive to any pressure, irrespective of the skin problems.

After staying overnight in Herat, an ancient city where the traffic consisted mostly of donkeys and camels, Lucy was forced to abandon wearing her prosthesis altogether as it was just too painful and uncomfortable. It now lay in the van, wrapped in its bin-bag covering, serving only as the secret repository for her remaining painkillers, codeine and morphine – there was no point in keeping cannabis there as they all openly used it, and Afghanistan was a major producer of it anyway.

Far from being upset at having to abandon wearing her leg, Lucy felt almost overwhelming relief. The wretched thing had become so uncomfortable, so smelly, so hot, so heavy, and so unbearably painful that without it – even though she still had the sores and the pain in her stump – she felt light and free. She no longer cared if people saw her on crutches. Showing her one-leggedness to the world was perfectly okay. After all, she was one-legged, so why should she hide what she was? However, along with her prosthesis, Lucy also abandoned wearing jeans, or preferring her loose cotton trousers (with left leg pinned up), or even looser long cotton skirts. On her foot she invariably wore a canvas high-ankle sneaker (usually referred to as a baseball boot) with a cotton sock, or, in very hot weather, an open strappy leather sandal, with her foot bare inside it.

From Herat they travelled to Kandahar, a bigger and slightly more modern city. Again they stayed in a hotel – the hotels in Afghanistan were so cheap that it wasn't worth sleeping in the van or the tent. Cannabis, or hashish as it was more commonly called there, was available everywhere in the country, and they all took to smoking chillums – short clay pipes – as cigarette papers were scarce.

Lucy and Jessica were exclusively vegetarian, and the others, while they would eat anything, usually preferred either chicken or vegetarian dishes. Afghanistan was not a vegetarian country, but a form of porridge, flatbreads, and apricots were readily available, so they didn't starve.

From Kandahar they continued their journey, the old VW occasionally breaking down temporarily, but able to be quickly fixed – increasingly by Davy rather than Zak, who was spending rather more time in a heroin-induced stupor. Lucy's concern for him increased with every day.

Eventually they arrived in Kabul. The city was at a high elevation in the Hindu Kush, surrounded by snow-covered peaks. Although the air was no longer hot, Lucy and Jessica both felt sick, with severe headaches. Kevin told them it was probably altitude sickness.

They stayed in the Zigi Hotel on what was commonly known as Freak Street, a street of shops selling wares almost entirely to the numerous hippies who passed through – goatskin Afghan coats (hairy side in, forming shaggy hair fringes at the edges and cuffs), embroidered kaftans, strings of coloured beads, water pipes, leather items, brass items, and – of course – hashish and all the paraphernalia for smoking it.

Both Lucy and Jessica felt too sick to do any shopping or to enjoy the ambience of the place, and could hardly wait to get on the road and descend to a lower altitude. The rest of the party bought various items and acquired considerable amounts of hashish, to smoke themselves but also to trade or – if they got no further opportunity – to smuggle back to England.

Lucy, except for crutching to the bathroom, lay on her bed in the hotel, suffering cracking headaches and constant nausea throughout the few days they stayed in Kabul, and Jessica wasn't much better. The good thing for Lucy was that, without her prosthesis, most of her sores started to heal, except for one bad ulcer close to the scar, which refused to scab over. Mandy acted as nurse, carefully washing Lucy's stump, dabbing it with disinfectant, and dressing the recalcitrant ulcer every day with clean, if not sterile, dressings that she managed to get in the city, held on with sticky Elastoplast strapping.

From Kabul they proceeded down the Kabul Gorge to Jalalabad, and thence to the Pakistan border. More money, albeit a small amount, changed hands at the border in the form of an exit tax. They then proceeded via the famous Khyber Pass, down a road with precipices on one side and numerous hairpin bends, to Peshawar for an overnight stay, and thence via Rawalpindi to Lahore, where they again stayed overnight in a hotel, and then drove on to the border with India. Both Jessica and Lucy felt much better as the altitude decreased. Actually Kabul was not at sufficient altitude to cause mountain sickness, which is usually only triggered at altitudes in excess of ten thousand feet, so their illness was in all probability caused by an infection. However, the apparent fact that these two suffered from mountain sickness, combined with the fact that it was almost winter, and bitterly cold in the mountains, altered the group's plans, which had originally been to head to Kathmandu in Nepal (albeit that Kathmandu was not at as high an altitude as Kabul). Instead, they proposed to head first to Amritsar, then to Delhi, before travelling on to Hardwar and Rishikesh (Zak's preference, the 'spiritual' trail), then heading back via Delhi to Agra to see the Taj Mahal, and then go to west to Bombay (as it still was named at the time, since renamed Mumbai), before finally heading to Goa.

CHAPTER ELEVEN

India – Part One

L ucy found India more relaxed than Pakistan, although the people, food, poverty, overcrowding and smells were much the same.

In Amritsar they visited the Golden Temple complex, or Sri Harmandir Sahib, or Sri Darbar Sahib, the holiest place in the Sikh religion. As well as admiring the fabulous architecture, they, along with the thousands of other visitors, were given a delicious free vegetarian meal. The Golden Temple stood in the middle of a man-made rectangular lake, surrounded by a white marble temple complex. The Golden Temple was reached by a covered causeway, and the Temple itself was covered in gold leaf, and shone spectacularly in the sunshine.

Lucy found the simple, welcoming, non-judgemental attitude of the people, both those working in the Temple and the thousands of worshippers, and the obvious spirituality of the place, very moving. Visitors of all nationalities, ages, and all faiths or none were equally welcomed, although, of course, the vast majority were Sikhs. If anyone stared at the pretty young hippy girl with only one leg, getting around on her crutches, Lucy certainly didn't notice it.

From there, they visited the nearby Jallianwala Bagh, a small park, and the site of a massacre in 1919 by British Indian troops under the command of British General Dyer on unarmed crowds attending a peaceful but, according to British rule at the time, unlawful protest against the arrest of two Indian Nationalists. In a different way, this was also very moving.

They stayed overnight in Amritsar, and the next day drove to Ambala, for another overnight stop. The roads were crowded, noisy, smelly and filled with all manner of vehicles and animals – busses, trucks, old cars (not so many), tuk-tuks, motorbikes, scooters and mopeds, bicycles, camels, cows, donkeys, goats, and even on one occasion an elephant. Some of the busses and trucks were garishly decorated, with pictures of Hindu deities (Krishna, Shiva, Ganesh, etc.), and strung with garlands of marigolds, with coloured tassels and fringes, and the busses often had piles of luggage and bicycles on the roof, and sometimes even passengers. India, like the UK, supposedly drives on the left of the road, but this was only tacitly observed, and then really only on the highways. In the towns and villages both vehicles and animals went where they pleased, and where they could find a space to squeeze into.

Beggars were everywhere, many living in absolute destitution and appalling squalor. Lucy noticed that many were scarred or disabled, quite a few with amputations, and she started to realise why no-one took any notice of her on her crutches. The beggars obviously felt that the western hippies, in their old VW van, were fabulously wealthy, and Lucy realised that, by comparison, they were. However there were simply too many beggars to give handouts to, even had they been millionaires, without the benefactors ending up as destitute as the recipients.

The impact of all this was almost overwhelming, an assault on both the senses and the sensibilities, and deeply troubling. Even Davy, normally either the hard-headed practical man or the wisecracking funny guy, was silent and thoughtful. All three girls at various points in the journey, had tears in their eyes – Lucy pretending to wipe her glasses with her handkerchief.

From Ambala, the following day, the journey continued to Delhi.

Delhi as a whole was a microcosm of all Indian cities – hot, smelly, noisy, crowded and seething with life. New Delhi, a small part of Delhi, by contrast, was a reflection of the British Raj – colonial India – with wide streets, parks, and imposing administrative buildings. The layout and many of the older buildings were designed by Sir Edwin Lutyens, an English pre-war architect of many grand and magnificent colonial-era buildings around the world.

They stayed in a cheap hotel, visited India Gate and some of the sights of New Delhi, visited Hindu temples, Sikh gurdwaras, Moslem mosques, ate street food (sometimes with bad consequences in the form of 'Delhi belly' – gastric upsets), and bought hashish. Davy and Zak also bought heroin, Davy to smuggle, Zak to use.

After a few days in Delhi, they drove north, to Hardwar and Rishikesh on the River Ganges (sacred in Hinduism), following in the spiritual path set by The Beatles, visiting more temples and ashrams (although they avoided the ashram of Maharishi Mahesh Yogi, as did most hippies following the very public falling-out between him and The Beatles). They saw – and listened to discourses by – gurus, yogis and various 'holy' men, and watched 'aarti' ceremonies – where Hindu priests or holy men would stand before a shrine – usually of Krishna, sometimes other deities – swaying a metal tray (steel or brass) decorated with lit ghee 'candles' (wicks of cotton dipped in ghee), flowers, and sometimes incense, while chanting bhajans (religious or spiritual chants).

Lucy noted the fervour of many of the devotions and accepted that there was a degree of spirituality about much of it, but she did not feel any particular desire to follow the teachings of any of these gurus or yogis. The others simply used the excuse to get stoned. Lucy, increasingly, used hashish only to deal with the ever-increasing pain in her stump, trying to avoid codeine, morphine or opiates of any sort except *in extremis*, as she daily saw the adverse effects of addiction in Zak.

After a few days, they drove south again, and skirting Delhi went on to Agra. There, of course, they saw the Taj Mahal, the universal symbol of India, and one of the most beautiful examples of classic Islamic architecture anywhere. They visited it by day, and also saw it by moonlight from their hotel.

In Agra there was a discussion as to where they should go next. Kevin and Mandy wanted to go east to Benares (Varanasi) to see the burning ghats, where many devout Hindus took the bodies of their deceased family members to be cremated on funeral pyres, lit at dawn, along the bank of the Ganges, before consigning the ashes to the river at dusk. Davy and Jessica wanted to turn southwest and visit Bombay (Mumbai) and then head south to the beaches of Goa, where, although hashish was not produced, it was readily available. Lucy was ambivalent, Zak too out of it to care.

Jessica produced an English copy of the I Ching, an ancient Chinese oracle, which could be consulted by throwing yarrow stalks, or using coins. She consulted this (using coins), and announced that she was sure that what it said indicated they should go west. The others weren't convinced, but after further discussion agreed that, because 'Gypsy Rose', their old VW camper, was getting pretty decrepit, they should probably head southwest to Bombay, where there was more chance of fixing it. Lucy expressed interest in looking at the I Ching, and Jessica lent it to her.

From Agra they travelled to Jaipur, saw the famous Red Fort, and stayed overnight in yet another cheap hotel. Continuing from there, starting very early in the morning, they drove all day, covering more than 400 miles, through the arid plains of Rajasthan and then into Gujerat, reaching Ahmedabad very late in the evening. They stayed two nights in Ahmedabad, recovering from this gruelling drive, before continuing the further 320 miles to Bombay (Mumbai). They reached the outskirts of Bombay when the engine in the old van started making loud knocking noises. They just about made it into the centre of the city when it gave out altogether. Too late in the evening to do anything, they found a hotel, and the next morning Davy checked out the van.

"It's defunct," he announced to the others. "The engine has blown. It needs a new engine, but we don't have the resources for that."

"How are we to get to Goa?" asked Mandy.

After making some enquiries, it transpired that the cheapest and easiest way to get to Goa was by ferry. Two old steamers, the *Konkan Shakti* and the *Konkan Sevak*, plied this route.

They spent a couple of days in Bombay, a huge city, with the part near the port full of grand buildings from the British Raj era (the General Post Office, the History Museum, the Railway Station, the Bombay High Court, the Taj Mahal Palace Hotel, and, of course, the Gateway of India arch, facing the entrance to the harbour).

Neither Lucy nor Zak spent much time sightseeing – Lucy because she was in too much pain, her stump getting more painful by the day, although she said little of this to the others, and Zak because he was spending too much time in a heroin-induced trance.

Tickets for the ferry were purchased at the wharf at the bottom of Dockyard Road. Because the van was defunct, the group had to abandon it, along with anything they couldn't carry. Lucy realised that her prosthetic leg, which she was now totally unable to wear, would have to be left behind. She extracted the contents of her secret compartment within it, stashing them in the cotton tote bag that she had acquired in one of the many markets along the way. Davy was also forced to sell quite a bit of the considerable quantity of hashish he had bought for smuggling, but kept the heroin.

Another item Lucy had to leave behind was her wooden box toilet seat. However, she had worked out by now that, if she placed her crutches in the right position, and lowered herself onto them in such a way that the handles were under her armpits (like very short axillary crutches), she *could* squat over a toilet hole.

The ferry left at 10am and took some 24 hours to get to Goa. At the dock, once the gates opened, the crowd with tickets rushed to the gangway to stake their places on the open decks, seated on life rafts. Davy, Mandy, Kevin and Jessica joined the rush, and bagged places for both themselves and for Lucy and Zak, neither of whom was able to rush.

The boat chugged its way out of the harbour, affording a good view of the Gate of India, and made its way slowly along the coast. Sellers on board offered drinks, guitars were produced and music played, and a festive communal spirit prevailed. At lunchtime a Goan fish curry with rice was served. Despite her vegetarian principles, Lucy ate, too hungry to refuse. Passengers who wanted to then played 'house' (bingo). From time to time, at various ports along the way, the boat hove to, and rowing boats came out from shore to deliver or collect embarking or disembarking passengers. Evening came, and a flaming sunset over the Arabian Sea. Then dinner was served – this time Lucy stuck to what vegetarian food was available. After dinner some of the Goans, many of whom were Roman Catholic (after several centuries as a Portuguese colony), began reciting the rosary, and Lucy was instantly transported back in memory to her childhood and her Irish Catholic upbringing. She suddenly realised that the incessant recitation of Hail Marys produced much the same effect as Hindu mantras such as "Om mani padme hum" or "Hare Krishna".

Then the life rafts became beds upon which people stretched out for the night.

The next morning, the boat was steaming past the beaches of north Goa, what Lucy would later come to know as Anjuna and Calangute, then further on the boat entered the Mandovi River, and finally docked at Panjim.

Having disembarked, the group hired two tuk-tuks to take them to Anjuna Beach, where, after some local enquiries and negotiations, they hired a beach house at a very cheap rate for a period of one month. This was in mid-December 1973.

Goa was somewhat different to most of the rest of India. For more than 400 years it had been a Portuguese colony, and the influence was still hugely apparent – in the architecture, the food, and the number of Catholic churches. It was not so crowded as many parts of India. Anjuna Beach, together with Calangute Beach slightly further south, was the centre of the Goa hippy scene. Many hippies lived in rented beach houses (there were virtually no hotels at that time), smoked pot, swam or lay around in the sun, bought and sold things in the local flea market, and had numerous parties on the beach – especially at full moon. There were even nude bathing parties.

Lucy, although she enjoyed the sun and the beach, and the laid-back atmosphere, tended to avoid the parties and the 'scene'. She occasionally sat on the beach, or visited the flea market. At Christmas she even went to mass in one of the Catholic churches, feeling that, as she had been in mosques, temples, gurdwaras and ashrams, she might as well cap it off with revisiting her own original religious roots. The service was so familiar to her, and yet exotically different in this setting. Although she felt no desire to re-embrace Catholicism, she took the opportunity to pray for resolution to Zak's addiction.

The regular beach scene, the nude bathing and the parties did not attract her. She was self-conscious of showing herself without a full covering of clothes – especially as her stump was swollen, and she had to keep the ever more painful ulcer on it covered with dressings and bandages. She remembered with nostalgia how wonderful it had felt to go swimming when they had stopped in Kavala, in Greece, early in the journey. She was also increasingly concerned about Zak. He was emaciated, his skin sallow, his strength rapidly dwindling.

This culminated in a day in very early January when, as usual, he had 'shot up' – injected himself with heroin – and he subsequently became delirious, broke into a sweat, and started raving, his eyes wild. Then violent shivering set in, despite the heat of the day. In the early stages of this Lucy, beside herself with fear, screamed for Jessica or Mandy to fetch help. After a few minutes a lanky young man with long tousled blond hair and beard arrived.

"Hi, I'm Pete. I graduated from medical school before I came out here."

Pete squatted down and looked at Zak, and took his pulse. Rising, he shook his head.

"Bad batch. I doubt he'll make it."

The whole group – Lucy, Davy, Kevin, Mandy and Jessica, plus Pete the medical graduate, sat with Zak throughout the long hours as his shivering got weaker, and he passed from delirium to unconsciousness.

Lucy was in turmoil. She had never consciously been deeply in love with Zak (nor he with her), but she had become fond of him despite his obvious faults. He had been the original driving force behind the trip, and certainly he was the prime reason she had come. He had also accepted her unreservedly after her accident. When she thought that, with only one leg, she would never be sexy or attractive for any man again, he had simply accepted her as the same pretty, sexy girl that had attracted him in the first place, and some place in Lucy's heart would always be eternally grateful to him for that.

Later Zak's breathing became hoarse. In the early hours of the morning, in the light of an oil lamp, stretched out on his charpoy in the little wooden beach house with its palm-thatched roof, Zak breathed out his last.

"He's gone, man," Pete said.

For Lucy, the next few days were a living nightmare. She took no part in arranging for disposal of the body, or funeral. Zak's image, etched in her memory, became a constant reminder of the potential consequences of their actions. The illicit trade, once seen as a reckless adventure, now revealed its ruthless, devastating potential. It wasn't simply a game anymore. It was an extremely dangerous game of chance, with potentially devastating consequences. This wasn't just about money or adventure; this was about lives, about morality, about choices. The realisation struck her with the force of a physical blow. She couldn't continue. She couldn't be a part of this any longer. The weight of the heroin, the potential for harm, was far more than she could bear.

Along with this, the sore, or ulcer, on her stump that had refused to heal, was giving her absolute hell, along with the area that was incredibly painful to press upon. She suspected that the sore was badly infected, but no matter what she did by way of antiseptic lotions, it failed to get any better. She vaguely considered asking Pete, the "qualified medical graduate" (which she took to mean he had completed his degree as a doctor, but never worked as a hospital intern or junior doctor). However, he was clearly a friend of Davy's, and she increasingly did not trust Davy, so she said nothing.

And then there were the nightmares. Vivid, terrifying dreams that haunted her sleep, filled with shadowy figures and whispered threats. She'd wake in a cold sweat, her heart pounding, the image of a dark, swirling vortex burned into her mind. These unsettling visions, coupled with the palpable tension in the house, fuelled a growing sense of dread.

CHAPTER TWELVE

India – Part Two

✠

Then one day, Davy confronted Lucy.

"Now we no longer have the van, so smuggling quantities of cannabis back is not an option. But we always had a second line of business, with heroin. The question was always how we were going to conceal it. We thought about putting it inside the acoustic guitars, but it's the first place they'll look.

"I know you kept a small supply of dope and painkillers inside your fake leg, and at one time it seemed that would be a good hiding place. Oh, don't look so surprised. I've seen you doing it. Zak didn't know, but the rest of us did. But then you stopped wearing the leg. But your crutches are hollow tubes. No reason not to put it in there. I reckon we can get about half a kilo into your crutches – and it should get us tens of thousands of pounds back in England. The police and customs are hardly going to hit on a disabled girl with only one leg.

"So, we need you to do this, Lucy."

Lucy was horrified.

"You want to smuggle heroin, after what happened to Zak? And you want *me* to be the fall guy if it goes wrong? How could you?"

"What happened to Zak was unfortunate, but, hey, he was responsible for his own destruction. This is business. Come on, Lucy, we need this. Nothing will go wrong, and you'll get your share of the proceeds."

"I absolutely refuse. I couldn't do it, not after all that's happened."

"Lucy, you don't have a choice. You will do it. How the hell else do you think you'll get back to England? And what else would you do? Just look at you – a one-legged hippy girl who couldn't go anywhere without help. So, I say you'll do this, and you cannot refuse. We need the money."

"Blood money," Lucy said, and crutched away, her tote bag over her shoulder. Davy watched her go, thoughtfully.

She was both absolutely furious, and completely terrified. In tears she wandered, not caring where she was going, thinking only of Davy's callousness and his threatening tone, and remembering Zak in his last hours, a thin, shaking, desperate figure, knowing that his time was up.

How could they do this, she thought to herself. How *could* they? But she knew they could and would. She wanted no part of it, but how was she to avoid being part of it? Apparently, she was key to their plans. Somehow, she had to get away. Escape from them. Make her own way home. But how? Davy was right – she was a one-legged hippy girl with a badly infected stump, who couldn't go anywhere or do anything much without help from other people. And if she tried to escape she could instantly be followed. There were no other one-legged British hippy girls with red hair and glasses wandering around Goa, so everyone who saw her would instantly remember it and tell them where she went. Her thoughts were in a whirl. Pain seared through both her mind and her body – the unhealed ulcer on her stump felt white hot, and, probably from the growing infection in it, she knew she was starting to run a fever.

She found herself passing through the flea market. As usual it was a busy scene, with colourful stalls selling clothing, ornaments, hashish (charas from the north, ganja from Kerala), street food, and all sorts of odds and ends. Suddenly she noticed a man walking through the market. It wasn't so much the appearance of the man that struck her, though that was notable – he was an Indian, tall and good-looking, with long, wavy black hair and a beard, wearing a saffron dhoti and kurta, which marked him out as a sanyasi – a renunciate holy man. What was remarkable was that, although the flea market was all bustle and noise, around this man, as he walked, was an aura of complete stillness and calm. He came towards Lucy, stopped, and looked at her.

"You are greatly troubled. Come." Although he spoke with a strong Indian accent, his English was good.

He turned and walked on. Without knowing why, Lucy felt compelled to follow him. She remembered all the gurus and sanyasis she had seen in Hardwar and Rishikesh, and somehow this man had made a far greater impression on her. He led her to a garden in front of a small white-washed, palm-thatched bungalow with a shady veranda. Several people, mostly Indians but including a few western hippies, were gathered in the garden, and as he approached they all folded their hands, bowed their heads to him and murmured, "Namaste, Swami-ji."

The man, addressed as 'Swami-ji', took off his shoes and sat cross-legged on a cushion at the top of the veranda steps, and everyone gathered around below and sat on the grass in front of him. Lucy slipped her arms out of her crutches and sat, too. He spoke.

"My dear brothers and sisters, I will speak in English, so our guests from the west can understand. You come to India seeking hashish and enlightenment. But enlightenment is not found in India, or in drugs. It is already within each of you, waiting for you to discover it.

"The nature of this world is duality – good and bad, right and wrong, beauty and ugliness, happiness and sadness, past and future. All these things are transitory, illusory.

"Many people seek happiness from gaining wealth and possessions. But material things can *never* bring true happiness. All material things are impermanent. When you are poor, you worry when and how you will get your next meal, and when you are rich you worry that someone will steal your wealth, or that your house will burn down, or your bank go bankrupt. So there is no happiness or true contentment there.

"You seek truth in religions. But all religions argue, 'This way is right, all the others are wrong.' Christians believe that by believing in Christ they will attain heaven. But what of those who never heard of Christ, or who were simply brought up in another religion? Do you think a just God will punish them? Moslems believe that by praying five times a day, facing Mecca, they will attain paradise. And if you do not pray five times each day, or do not know in which direction Mecca is located? We Hindus usually believe that we will be reborn, in a cycle of birth, death and rebirth, and the good or evil we do will be rewarded or punished in next lifetime. But nobody remembers previous life, so what is point of punishment, if you do not know for what you are punished?

"My friends, all these things are an illusion, maya, a trap. You are victim of circumstances. As for past and future – past is past, gone, it cannot come back. Future has not happened, so is also an illusion. Only the present moment is real. Do not regret what has past, good or bad, and do not either dream of the future or fear what may happen. Live each moment, breath by breath, as only this moment is real.

"It is like this. You go to cinema – watch a film. You see characters on film do funny things, you laugh. Sad things happen in film, you cry. But all the time, you know it is just a film – it is not real. There is a greater reality. Life is also like this. We are rich or we are poor, we are men or we are women, we are high caste or we are untouchable, we are Indian or we are western, we are old or we are young, we are fit and strong, or we are sick or disabled – makes no difference. Inside each of us is the spark of the divine. Find that, and everything else is like the cinema film, to be enjoyed but not taken as reality.

"Even the people we love, our family, our friends, our parents, our children, our partners, are transitory. Relationships can end, friends can turn away, people can walk out of our lives, or they can die." Here, he looked directly at Lucy. "So we need to find a centre of our being that is not transitory or illusory, that is always with us, within us, from our first breath to our last.

"What traps us is attachment. It is not that friends, family, wealth or possessions are bad. But our attachment to them catches us, and causes us suffering. Learn to enjoy what this world offers without attachment.

"So seek the ultimate truth, that which cannot be taken away from you, because it is what gives life to you. Look for the divine within yourself."

He stood up, and folded his hands in blessing. Those in the garden got up, folded their hands and bowed their heads, and most of them left. Lucy slowly got up, reaching for her crutches.

"You." He beckoned to her. "Come."

She went to the veranda steps, and made her way up them.

Her turned to go inside. Lucy followed, stopping momentarily to take off her sandal. She was, by now, used to doing this in mosques, temples and even some homes.

Inside was a hall with a few doors off it. The Swami went through the first one, Lucy following. Inside was a shady sitting room, with rattan chairs. Open widows with slatted shutters let in a scent of jasmine and hibiscus, which mingled with that of incense. In the middle of the ceiling a fan slowly turned. The Swami sat in one of the rattan chairs and beckoned Lucy to sit in the other.

"I am Swami Yogananda, and this is the ashram provided for me by some of my students," he said. "So tell me, what troubles you? It is not just that you have the disability, the missing leg, or that you are sick."

"No," said Lucy, amazed at his insight in knowing she was unwell. Not knowing quite why, she proceeded to tell him about Zak and the others, and the journey to India, and what had happened to Zak, and Davy's proposition, and how she could neither go through with it nor see a way out of it, and how she probably had an infected sore on her stump, and maybe she might die anyway. In passing, she also mentioned that she could possibly try and contact Brian, in the hospital in Bangalore.

"Ah!" he exclaimed. "You want to keep clean conscience. It's good, but you need two things. On the practical level, you need means of escape from these people. Maybe, if you can get there, this Brian friend in Bangalore can assist you. On deeper level, you need point of sanctuary within yourself, where you can always go, no matter what happens.

"I know someone who may assist with first part. I will go and speak to her. Wait here, I will return and we will deal with second part." He got up and left the room. Lucy sat and waited a few minutes until he returned.

"I have asked someone to come and assist you with practical issues. She has gone to get necessary items and will be here later.

"Now we will talk of more important things. Within you, Lucy, as within all of us, is power of life. Your breath comes into you unbidden, and leaves you unbidden. You can only hold breath for short time, then it comes regardless. Is a power greater than you, but is within you.

"Sit quietly, be still, let go of pain, let go of grief, let go of thoughts – they will come, but let them go. Close the eyes. Focus on your breath. Breathe in and feel universal life flow into you. Breathe out and let yourself become one with universe. Every breath, follow it in, and follow it out. Every time thoughts come and distract you, let them go, and come back to the breath.

"Do this regularly, every day, maybe twice a day, for at least half an hour – an hour if you can. And do it every time you feel upset or in need of comfort. Know that whatever happens to you, life itself loves you and cares for you, and nothing else matters.

"Do this now, while I go and check on person who may provide the practical help."

He again rose and left the room. Lucy sat, with her eyes closed, and tried to focus on her breath. The stillness and peacefulness of her surroundings helped, and soon she felt incredibly calm and at peace within herself, despite the fact that, as the Swami had said, her thoughts continued to come and go – memories of Zak, questions about how she could escape... Each time she became aware that she was thinking these things, she consciously refocussed on her breath. Even the intensity of the burning pain in her stump, although it was still there, ceased to bother her so much.

After half an hour he came back with a young Indian woman, not much older than Lucy, dressed in the usual sari.

"Lucy, this is Lakshmi Banerjee. She will help you. She speaks good English. I will leave you to discuss with her what you can do on the practical level."

He turned to leave. As he did so, Lakshmi bent briefly and touched his feet.

Turning back to Lucy, Lakshmi looked at her.

"Show me the sore on your amputated leg."

Lucy pulled up her skirt, revealing her stump, looking rather red and swollen. She tore off the dressings over the ulcer. It was inflamed, and oozing a sticky, cloudy mucus with a putrid smell.

"Yes, it is badly infected. I can give you temporary treatment that will help, but you will need to see a doctor within two days, no more, or you will become so sick that you will most probably die. Wait, I will be back in two minutes."

She left the room, returning moments later with a basin, a jug of water, a jar of ointment, clean dressings and a bandage. As she set to work on Lucy's stump, bathing it, putting ointment on the ulcer and dressing it with a new sterile gauze dressing from a sealed paper packet, she asked Lucy to tell her the details of her story, which Lucy did, noticing, as she did so, that the pain in her stump had eased considerably, and that her head felt clearer. As Lucy finished her account, and Lakshmi finished bandaging her stump, Lakshmi said to Lucy: "So, Swami-ji mentioned you have friend in Bangalore, Brian? This Brian, he is doctor?"

"Yes. He works in a hospital in Bangalore."

"Ah, so. Is good. You must go to him. You need to be in hospital."

"But how?" Lucy asked. "He is in Bangalore, we are in Goa, it's hundreds of miles. I don't know if I can travel, and anyway, my companions will be looking for me, and if they think I am leaving they will most probably try and stop me."

"Do you have money and passport with you?"

"Yes." Lucy patted her cotton tote bag. "But almost everything else is at the house with my companions."

"You must leave everything else. And I can try to make it so they do not notice you leaving Goa. You will go on the train this evening. It is overnight, gets to Bangalore tomorrow morning. Before you go I will take you to Post Office where you can telephone or send telegram to this Brian, so he can meet you. But first I will need to disguise you, so your travelling companions cannot know where you have gone. We cannot give you the leg, so we must make you look like the disabled Indian girl. There are many Indians with amputations and other disabilities here, but not many western ones, so if you go undisguised it will be easy for them to find out and follow you. Better they don't know. Come with me."

Lakshmi led the way out of the house, pausing momentarily on the veranda while she put on her own sandals and Lucy put on her single one. They proceeded through the garden, to a smaller house hidden behind some bushes. Inside was an old but clean settee and a table.

"Sit."

Lucy sat. Lakshmi left and returned after a few moments with a variety of things, including an old pair of wooden underarm crutches.

"It is good you have the clip-on sunglasses on your glasses. Your eyes are too blue otherwise, so you must keep the sunglasses on, even when light goes. But your hair is too fair and too red. This is kohl." She produced a jar. "We use as eye makeup. But I will use to darken your hair."

She took kohl from the jar and rubbed it into Lucy's hair until it was virtually unrecognisable. She also darkened Lucy's eyebrows. Then she plaited Lucy's hair into a long pigtail, which she explained was the common way for Indian women to keep their hair tidy, and would also prevent too obvious revelation that it was coloured with kohl.

"Now, your skin is too light, and Indian girls don't have freckles, but I have bottle of the fake suntan."

She massaged the fake tan into Lucy's face, neck and ears, onto her hands and arms, around her waist, and over her foot and ankle, until Lucy's skin in all those places was an even brown.

"Now, we give you the tilak." So saying, Lakshmi took up a small jar of red paste, and with the tip of a finger placed the customary red dot between Lucy's brows. "And you must wear the sari." Lakshmi produced first a short, tight cotton tee-shirt, which Lucy pulled on, having taken off her loose kaftan and skirt; then came a coloured cotton sari.

"Sorry, but you must stand. You can hold onto me if you need."

Lucy stood, balancing on her leg and placing her hands on Lakshmi's shoulders, while Lakshmi expertly folded and wrapped the sari around Lucy's waist, tucking it in where appropriate to keep it in place, then crossways up over her breasts and left shoulder, bringing the loose end up over Lucy's head.

"Try to keep this over your head, at least until you are on train. It helps hide the hair. And make sure sari does not come loose. Now, you must be using these." Lakshmi picked up the wooden crutches, and slipped them under Lucy's arms. "No Indian girl needing crutches would have your short metal ones, unless she is from a city and is very modern and quite rich. Try walking with them."

Lucy, remembering to put her weight through her hands and sides, not through her armpits, walked around the room quite comfortably. Fortuitously they turned out to be practically the right height for her, without any need for adjustment.

"Good. Now, after we have got Swami-ji to give his blessing, we get the rickshaw to Post Office for you to contact Brian, and then we get taxi to railway station, and you get train to Bangalore."

Lakshmi helped Lucy to fold up her kaftan and skirt into a small pack, and put it in Lucy's tote bag.

"And those," Lucy pointed to her forearm crutches.

"Leave them. When you are at the hospital, or when you are back in England, you can get more."

With that, they left the building, and walked back through the garden. Swami Yogananda was on the veranda of his ashram. Lucy folded her hands, and bowed her head.

"Namaste, Swami-ji. I can find no words to express my thanks to you."

"Namaste. Go in peace, Lucy. Remember what I taught you. You are a child of God, and a spark of the divine is within you. Nurture its flame, focus on your breath, and the grace of God will protect you."

They left the garden and hailed a bicycle rickshaw. Lakshmi spoke to the driver, and he took them to the Post Office.

"Remember, do not speak to anyone except on telephone. If cannot get through we send the telegram. But try telephone first."

Lucy opened her wallet and took out the by now rather crumpled piece of card with Brian's contact details, and some loose coins. Following the instructions, she put money in the payphone and connected to the operator, giving the number for the hospital in Bangalore. Amazingly, she was put through without any bother.

"Could I speak to Dr Brian Patterson, please? He's a British doctor working there."

"Just a moment," said the voice at the other end. "Ah, yes. He is on duty now. I can put you through to his department. Who shall I say is calling?"

"Lucy Ryan. I'm a relative of his." Lucy stretched the truth to try and ensure she got to speak to Brian. "It's very important that I speak to him now."

"Okay. Hold, please."

A couple of clicks and buzzes ensued. Then a male voice, with a faint Irish accent, said, "Brian Patterson speaking."

Tears of relief sprang to Lucy's eyes as she told him who she was, and why she needed him.

"Can you meet me off the train from Goa, first thing in the morning, please Brian? Oh, and by the way, you'll get a shock when you see me. I'm disguised as an Indian."

Brian laughed. "That's okay, Lucy. I'll see you tomorrow. Have a good journey."

Lucy returned to Lakshmi.

"It's okay," she said. "I spoke to Brian, and he'll meet me at the station in the morning."

Lakshmi smiled. "Swami-ji told you that the grace would protect you. Come, let's go."

This time they hailed a motor taxi and Lakshmi gave instructions to the driver to take them to Madgaon Junction Railway Station.

"I wouldn't normally suggest it, but if you can afford it, get a first-class ticket. You are sick, and you need space and comfort."

"Thank you, Lakshmi. Yes, I have enough money for that."

They made their way to the ticket desk, and Lakshmi spoke to the clerk. Lucy, again taking out her wallet, handed her the money required.

"Okay. Here is your ticket – first-class. Train leaves at six p.m. It's now five-ten. Over there is stall selling juice and fruit." She pointed. "Get enough for journey. Do not drink water unless boiled. Here we part. Good luck, Lucy. It has been an honour to meet you."

"How can I ever thank you?" said Lucy, tears in her eyes. "Can I get in touch with you, when all this is over?"

"Yes, but do not thank me. Thank Swami-ji. And although we physically part, we are always together in spirit. Here…" So saying, Lakshmi took an old envelope out of her bag and scribbled her contact details on it. Lucy carefully put it in her wallet and put this into her bag, then threw her arms around Lakshmi, hugging her, nearly losing her crutches as she did so – Lakshmi grabbed them just in time, laughing.

"Go well, Lucy-ji. Namaste."

"Stay well, Lakshmi-ji. Namaste."

And so they parted. As instructed, Lucy bought juice and fruit, and made her way to the platform, which was like platforms in all Indian railway stations – crowded, noisy, smelly and seething with life.

In due course Lucy boarded her train. The first-class carriage, while not luxurious, was clean, comfortable, air-conditioned, and had lots of space and few passengers. Lucy sank back into a comfortable seat, leant her wooden crutches against the carriage wall beside her, closed her eyes, and tried to meditate as Swami-ji had instructed her, focussing on her breath. The train started to move, slowly at first, but soon picking up speed, quickly leaving Goa behind, and with it all that part of Lucy's life that it represented.

CHAPTER THIRTEEN

India – Part Three

❖

The train pulled into the station in Bangalore well before 8:00am the next morning. Lucy had spent the night alternately meditating and dozing. She had weird dreams, and knew she was running a fever, alternatively sweating and shivering. She was light-headed getting off the train, and might have fallen if another passenger had not come to her rescue and helped her descend to the platform.

Brian was at the station to meet her, and laughed when he saw her, but then became concerned when he realised just how ill she was. He helped her out of the station and into a taxi.

As the taxi threaded its way slowly through the morning traffic, Lucy brought Brian up to date on her story.

Eventually, the taxi pulled up at the hospital.

"Wait here," Brian said. He spoke to the taxi driver, then went into the hospital and came out again a minute later pushing an empty wheelchair.

"Lucy, sit in this. It'll be quicker and easier for you."

She was too tired and too sick to argue. Brian wheeled her into the building, along a corridor and into a cubicle in what Lucy later realised was the emergency department. He helped her onto a couch, and then spoke to a nurse, who disappeared off somewhere. Then, lifting the hem of her sari, he then examined Lucy's stump. After a moment, he called over another nurse, asking her to bring gloves and a kidney dish. Putting on the latex gloves, he gently unwrapped the bandage, and removed the dressing, depositing them in the kidney dish, which the nurse removed. The pain was intense as he did this, and Lucy clamped her jaw to prevent from crying. Her stump was swollen and inflamed, and the ulcer seemed to have grown wider and deeper, with dark red, yellow and black patches in it, and more of the foul discharge seeping from it.

"Ah, yes," he said. "It is very badly infected, but the ayurvedic ointment has helped slow down the infection. It will need to be debrided and washed out. The infection may have got into the bone, in which case we may need to deal with that too."

Lucy explained that, as well as the infected ulcer, there was an area of her stump that was extremely painful when pressed.

"Yes, I think you might have what is called a neuroma there. That is, where the nerve has been severed the end grows branches, like a tree. They are extremely sensitive to pressure, and send pain signals to the brain. I'm going to call a colleague to come and look at you."

He left the cubicle. A few minutes later a middle-aged Indian doctor appeared with Brian.

"Lucy, this is Mr da Souza. He is the best consultant general surgeon we have here. He trained in England, so he speaks perfect English. I have other patients I need to see, but I'll check on you later." Brian smiled at her, and left.

Mr da Souza asked Lucy about her symptoms, got a nurse to take her temperature and blood pressure, and then gently asked, "May I examine the site of the problem, please?"

"Of course," said Lucy, pulling up her sari to reveal her stump.

Mr da Souza felt carefully, and at various points Lucy could no longer prevent herself from audibly wincing and crying out in pain.

"As well as the infection, which is very bad, I am of the opinion that you have a large neuroma. It will need to be cauterised – cut out and sealed off so that it does not grow again. Also, I think that you may possibly have bone spurs growing at the end of the bone, or – perhaps worse – you may have osteomyelitis, causing the bone to splinter. An x-ray would confirm, but if we are going to operate, which we will have to do, we shall discover without need for an x-ray.

"Lucy, your residual leg is in very bad condition, and it may well be that we will need to do a revision. That is, we may need to shorten what remains, even up to your hip. In any case, we shall have to remove all the badly infected tissue."

"That's okay," said Lucy. "I can't wear a prosthesis as it is anyway. I just want to get better and live, even if all the rest of my leg has gone."

"That is good. Now, I will give you a local painkiller and I will get the nurses to bathe your residual leg, get you to a ward, get you cleaned up, and put you on IV antibiotics to control that infection. And tomorrow morning I will operate." He injected local anaesthetic into Lucy's hip, and the pain slowly eased as her stump went numb. A nurse sponged away the pus with disinfectant, prior to the other actions Mr da Souza had prescribed.

Brian came to see Lucy later that afternoon. She was in a clean hospital nightdress, lying on a bed in a comfortable and clean ward, and she herself had been cleaned – all traces of kohl and fake suntan removed. She had an IV drip into her left arm, with antibiotics, and she had been given painkillers and sedatives.

"Mr da Souza is lovely," she said. "But it doesn't seem to be an Indian name."

"He's originally from Goa, where you have just been," Brian replied. "I understand that his grandfather was a Portuguese merchant who settled there when it was a colony, and married a local girl."

"Ah, that explains it," said Lucy. "I wonder what I shall do if I get through all this."

"Of course you'll get through this," Brian replied, firmly. "And don't worry about later. We can talk about it when you are recovering."

"You're the second person in two days to tell me not to worry about the future. Only the present moment is real!" She laughed, then yawned. "I miss my violin. I'll need to get one to practice on."

"Yeah, sure. But time enough for that too. I'll come and see you sometime tomorrow, after you wake up from the surgery."

When Lucy did come fully awake the next day, after the surgery, Brian was only her second visitor. The first was Mr da Souza.

"So Lucy," Mr da Souza said, "I have good news and bad news. The good news is that you are out of danger and will make a good recovery. The bad news is that we had to remove the rest of your residual leg. There was very bad osteomyelitis in the femur – that is, an infection of the bone. It had probably been there since your accident, but initially dormant. But it was also feeding the infection in the ulcer – which is why it wouldn't heal. The bone was starting to splinter and disintegrate. You also had a bad neuroma. But all of that is gone now. We have given you what is called a hip disarticulation – that is, we had to remove all of your femur, up to the hip joint, and quite a lot of tissue including the neuroma and all the infected tissue. So you have no residual leg left on that side.

"There is a drain in your incision, which will come out in three or four days if all is well. Your stitches will take a bit longer. But apart from localised pain, you should start to feel much better within a day or two. Your fever is already going away.

"I have ordered necessary pain relief. If you need more, please let the nurses know. But there will be pain, though it will ease over time. However, as you have already had an amputation, you will know what to expect."

Mr da Souza was right – Lucy did start to feel better very quickly. By the time Brian came to see her she was fully awake, clear-headed, with no fever, and although her left hip was very sore, the intense burning pain she had previously had in her stump was gone. All that remained was her usual tingling feeling in the toes of her missing foot. Even her phantom pains seemed to have eased off.

"Well," she said to Brian, when he came to see her, "I came here with one-and-a-bit legs, and now the bit has gone."

"I know," said Brian. "But it'll be okay." He looked thoughtful for a moment, then laughed. "Do you remember that holiday we had when you were still a child and I was just out of school, when we went to the Isle of Man. We saw several Manx cats, and there were two varieties – stumpies, which had a residual tail, and rumpies, which had no tail at all. You've merely gone from being a stumpy to being a rumpy."

Lucy laughed. "I should be offended at that, but I'm not." She became serious. "Thank you, Brian, for getting me taken care of."

"You are most welcome. Of course I would take care of you. By the way, I've written to your mother to let her know what's happened."

"Thanks, Brian."

Over the next few days Brian was a frequent visitor to Lucy's bedside. In bits and pieces, leaving nothing out, she told Brian the full story of how and why she had come to India, how she had to abandon wearing her prosthesis, where the journey had taken her, and what happened to Zak. She then recounted the heroin-smuggling plans, how she wanted no part of it and had to leave, and about her encounter with Swami Yogananda, how profound it had been, and the assistance provided by Lakshmi.

Lucy once again found herself tethered to IV, drain, and catheter. The pain across her hip and groin was sharp, and increased slightly as the pain medication was gradually eased (at Lucy's insistence, as she was assiduously avoiding addiction) before it, too, started to ease, but it was never as severe as the pain Lucy had experienced immediately before her 'revision', as the amputation of her stump was termed.

She looked curiously at her fresh amputation when the bandages were removed and the drain taken out. A dark red line of new scar stretched across her hip, approximately following the line of her groin, with big stitches every centimetre or so. On either side of the scar the flesh was slightly swollen, but healthy looking. Below this, there was nothing. Effectively, Lucy's left buttock now curved under her pelvis and joined her abdomen in this line of scar and stitching. Her catheter was also removed, and she was allowed out of bed, and into a wheelchair.

Lucy wasn't sure how she felt about becoming a hip-level amputee. Over the previous weeks she had got used to not being able to wear her prosthesis, so the absence of her stump made little difference in terms of either her self-image or her mobility, as they had recently been. The most difficult part, initially, was sitting on the toilet. Her amputation site (she still thought of it as her stump, although there was no residual leg left) was still tender and, with no thigh on that side, she had to lean to her right so all the weight was on her right buttock and thigh, which was not exactly comfortable. She realised that, as she healed, this would become slightly less of an issue. Of course, prior to the operation she had hoped that, with time and healing, she would again be able to don her prosthesis and walk about on two legs, albeit with a limp. That prospect now seemed much less certain. However, she realised the impact on her was far less than that of her initial amputation.

A few days later her stitches were taken out, and Mr da Souza pronounced himself satisfied with her progress. Brian now effectively took over management of her rehabilitation, issuing her with a new pair of crutches – underarm or axillary ones, to be sure, but adjustable tubular metal ones, not the old wooden ones.

Despite the advice of both Swami Yogananda and Brian not to worry about the future, Lucy was concerned about what she would do when she left hospital. She would need to stay in Bangalore for at least a couple of weeks, to ensure she was fit enough to travel, but where? And then what? She probably had enough money to return to England by an overland bus from Delhi or Bombay, but she dreaded the prospect of such a journey now, with its inevitable hardships and discomforts, with people she didn't know, and with memories of Zak at every turn of the road.

Equally, what was she to do when she got back to England? She had lived with Zak before the journey to India started, and now that he was gone... Well? She supposed she would have to go and live in her mother's house again, but she didn't relish the prospect, much as she loved her mother. Even living there, she would be surrounded by memories – memories of Zak, of the band, of the carefree times she had – even after her first amputation.

"What am I going to do when they discharge me?" Lucy asked Brian. "I don't know Bangalore, I probably don't have enough money to rent anywhere to live – at least not for more than a couple of weeks, and somehow I'll need to get enough to get home to England. I suppose I will have to go to the Irish Embassy or the British High Commission and get myself repatriated."

"Absolutely not," Brian replied. "I rent a couple of rooms close to the hospital, and you can stay there as my guest. I finish my contract here in four weeks' time. I had thought of applying for a job in Sydney, in Australia, but I can equally well go back to Britain or Ireland, and I'll get you a ticket so we can travel together."

"Sydney? My father lives in Sydney. I have an open invitation to visit him. I never thought I would do so, but if you want to go and work in Sydney – why not?"

"Hm. Okay, we'll think about it. Don't rush into any hasty decisions."

But the more Lucy thought about it, the more she liked the idea. She had left England as an amputee with a residual limb on which she habitually wore a prosthesis. She had still tended to avoid going out in public on crutches. Now, as a hip-level amputee, she would have to use crutches.

Even if, at some stage (and not in India) she could be fitted with a prosthesis, she had learned enough at the prosthetic fitting centre to know that most hip-level amputees used crutches (or a wheelchair) for much if not all of the time, and even if they had a prosthetic leg, this use of crutches was out of preference or necessity. She had seen one girl, younger than her, who had been fitted with a hip-level prosthesis following amputation for bone cancer, and it was a cumbersome contraption with a bucket-shaped socket held on with a big strap round the waist with two buckles. At the front of the socket was a hinge, to which the usual pylon, knee and foot assembly was attached. The girl had no direct control over the leg, except by rotating her pelvis, and the resulting gait was slow and lopsided – anything but graceful. The girl had to take it off every time she went to the toilet.

In Australia, no-one apart from her father would know her. She had found, in India, a very satisfying degree of anonymity on her crutches. Perhaps this could continue in Australia, at least until she had gained sufficient self-assurance that it no longer mattered. And, if it was possible to be fitted with a prosthesis, Australia was as likely to be as good a place for it to happen as England, though she wasn't sure whether Australia had a free health service, or what the implications might be. But the biggest plus of all would be that she could find the space and time to come to terms with everything that had happened, without constant reminders of Zak.

She assiduously practised her meditation, not always easy in hospital where there was always activity of some sort – doctors' rounds, patients' blood pressure and temperature being taken and recorded, medications given out, meals, physio sessions, washing sessions, and so on. It certainly helped to keep her calm, and from worrying too much about her next moves.

A few more days, and Mr da Souza said to her, "Lucy, you have made very good progress. Your incision is healing well, there is no sign of infection, all your vital signs are normal, and I understand you are able to ambulate successfully on crutches. I see no reason to detain you here in hospital. I understand you will be staying with your friend Brian, so you will be in the care of not only a healthcare professional, but one who can expertly continue your rehabilitation. Therefore, I am discharging you. I wish you good health. Namaste!"

"Oh, Mr da Souza, thank you so much. I know your expertise has not only saved my life, but enabled me to make such a quick recovery. I can never thank you enough. Namaste."

She dressed herself in the kaftan and skirt she had taken off when Lakshmi disguised her as an Indian girl (she also had the sari, now washed and neatly folded, in her bag), put on her sandal, and as soon as Brian finished his morning shift, she accompanied him to his rooms, which were a five-minute walk from the hospital – though Lucy, out in public on her new underarm crutches for the first time, took rather longer, stopping to rest about halfway. She realised she had not yet regained her full strength, but knew it would come with time and exercise.

Brian had two rooms plus a small kitchen and bathroom. One of the rooms was his bedroom, but the other had a charpoy (a light bedframe with cotton-canvass webbing) scattered with cushions, as well as a table, two wooden chairs, and a cupboard with drawers down one side. A French window opened onto a balcony that extended to a similar window into Brian's room.

"Sorry, it's a bit sparse," Brian said, indicating the room. "I can provide sheets and blankets. And I have a few books if you need something to pass the time while I'm at work. There's even a radio, but it doesn't get any English-language stations, only Kannada, Telugu, Tamil and Hindi."

"This is luxury," Lucy said. "I'll be fine here. The only thing I really miss is not having a violin to play. But," she looked at her kaftan and skirt, "I'm going to have to get some clothes. The only change I have is the sari I wore on the train."

"Are those the only clothes you have?" asked Brian.

"Yes. I left everything except what I had with me. I'll have to get some new clothes as soon as possible. I don't even have a change of underwear."

"There's one of the nurses at the hospital, Sita, who lives in a flat upstairs," Brian said. "I'll ask her to call in and get her to obtain what you need. Wait here, I'll go and see if she's in. I don't think she's on shift at present."

He left, returning a few minutes later with a young Indian woman that Lucy recognised as one of the nurses who had been on her ward on occasion in the hospital.

Brian opened his wallet and took out a roll of rupees, handing them to Lucy.

"Brian, I don't need…"

"We can sort it out later," he interrupted. "You are virtually family, so at least let me look after you for now."

Lucy blushed, and murmured her thanks.

"Now you and Sita can discuss what you need, and she can get it for you. It is probably best that you don't go out yet; you got quite tired on the way here, and it's not that long ago you had major surgery, following a very nasty infection."

"Yes, sir!" said Lucy, saluting, which made them all laugh.

Then Brian went to do some grocery shopping, and Lucy and Sita discussed clothing and female hygiene products. Lucy had been given a nightdress, a comb and a toothbrush by the hospital, but she had nothing else except what she had in her tote bag when she left the house in Goa. This consisted, apart from her sari, of her spare glasses, glasses case and clip-on sunglasses, her small sketchpad and some pencils, a hairbrush, a small compact, a nail file, lip salve, a hanky, an almost empty small bottle of cologne, a smaller bottle of patchouli oil, a box of matches and a packet with eight unsmoked cigarettes (she hadn't had one since leaving Goa), a plastic packet with about one ounce of hashish, eleven codeine capsules and most of the morphine she had been prescribed in Afghanistan, half a dozen tampons, the copy of the I Ching that Jessica had lent her, her wallet containing rupees, travellers' cheques, and the pieces of paper with contact details for Brian, her father, and Lakshmi, and her Irish passport.

Having discussed her needs, Sita left to go shopping for Lucy. Going to the kitchen, Lucy found coffee and a kettle, and decided to make herself a cup. She found that, by doing the forbidden thing and resting her weight through the armpit and the saddle of one of her crutches, she could carry the cup – and it was easier to do than it had been with her forearm crutches. She took the coffee to the balcony, where there were two folding chairs, and sipped it, watching the street below, teeming with all the bustle typical of all Indian cities. She decided to smoke one of her cigarettes. In her own mind, she had decided that, when the present pack was finished, she would not smoke any more, but for now, sipping her coffee and inhaling the smoke, she felt content simply enjoying it.

She had just finished her coffee and cigarette when Brian returned. He packed away his shopping in the kitchen.

"I got vegetable samosas for lunch," he said. "I remembered that you are vegetarian. I eat very little meat myself, these days, just a bit of chicken or fish sometimes. And there are some mangos and bananas. I see you've had coffee."

They had lunch sitting on the balcony. Then Brian had to leave for his afternoon shift. As he did so, Sita returned. She had a bag from which she produced three cotton tee-shirts, two mid-calf-length brightly coloured cotton skirts, a pair of thin multi-coloured cotton bloomers, a pair of jeans, four pairs of panties, four bras, cotton pyjamas, a pack of sanitary pads, another toothbrush and toothpaste, shampoo, a bottle of rosewater, a pack of tissues, a small sewing kit (with scissors, needles, thread in various colours, pins, and safety pins), and, last but not least, a big cotton bag with a shoulder strap, into which Lucy could pack everything if she needed to. Lucy thanked Sita profusely. She spent the afternoon trying on clothes, looking at herself in the bathroom mirror, and trying to decide whether to pin up the empty left legs of the pyjamas, bloomers and jeans, or cut them off and sew them.

She decided to cut and sew, and over the next couple of days she snipped and sewed until all three were tailored to snugly fit her 'stump'. She had no prosthesis, and there was no point trying to hide the level of her amputation. She kept the excess fabric in case she needed to patch, or to make anything else out of it.

Later, as she waited for Brian to return, she practised her meditation, and, although she still grieved for Zak, she felt calm and at peace with everything that had happened.

Lucy settled easily into Brian's 'rooms'. The bathroom had a toilet, basin and shower, but no bath. However, Lucy had long since got used to balancing on her one leg in the shower. Of course, a shower seat or grab bars on the wall would have made it easier, but she was okay without these refinements. Brian, as a doctor, was very aware of her potential needs, and within a few days acquired a folding wooden shower stool for her. In the kitchen Lucy either sat on a stool, or moved around on her crutches. Brian was a reasonable cook, and street food was also readily available.

Over the next few days Lucy and Brian discussed the options for when his contract ended. Lucy was keen on the idea of going to Australia. Brian, remembering that her father had walked out on his family, was less convinced.

Lucy remembered Jessica consulting the I Ching, and she decided to try it. Thinking about the question of whether they should go to Australia, using three coins, she them six times, allocating a score of 3 to heads and 2 to tails. The first throw produced three tails, i.e. a score of 6, which indicated a broken changing bottom line for the hexagram. The next throw was 3 heads, a score of 9, which equated to a changing solid line. The third throw also produced three heads, a 9, and a changing solid line. The fourth and fifth throws were both three tails, so two more broken changing lines were added. The final throw produced 2 heads and 1 tail, a score of 8, and an unchanging broken line.

The hexagram thus produced looked like this:

Lucy looked this up in the table at the end of the book, and found that it represented Hexagram 46, entitled SHENG, PROMOTION. She quickly found the relevant text, and read:

HEXAGRAM 46
SHENG ASCENDING, PROMOTION
Component trigrams:

Below: Sun, wind, wood, bland, mild.

Above: Kun, earth, female, passive, etc.

TEXT Ascending. Supreme success! It is essential to see a great man, so as to banish anxiety. Progressing towards the south brings good fortune.

COMMENTARY ON THE TEXT At the proper time, the weak ascend. Gentleness and willing acceptance are conjoined. A firm line is central (to the lower trigram) and wins response; hence great success is foretold. What is said about the freedom from anxiety to be gained from visiting a great man indicates that in this way blessings will be attained. Going south brings good fortune in the sense that it will lead to the fulfilment of what is willed.

SYMBOL This hexagram symbolizes trees growing upwards from the earth. The Superior Man most willingly accords with virtuous Ways; starting from small things, he accumulates a great heap (of merit).

The Lines

6 FOR THE BOTTOM PLACE Certainty of promotion— great good fortune!

COMMENTARY This is because the will of our superiors accords with our own.

9 FOR THE SECOND PLACE Full of faith, he performed the summer sacrifice.

COMMENTARY The faith (or confidence) indicated by this line leads to great happiness.

9 FOR THE THIRD PLACE He was promoted (to office) in a larger city.

COMMENTARY This line indicates that we cause no doubts (to arise in the minds of others).

6 FOR THE FOURTH PLACE The King sacrificed on Mount Chi— good fortune and no error!

COMMENTARY This indicates our willing compliance (with duty, tradition, circumstances, etc.)

6 FOR THE FIFTH PLACE Righteous persistence brings good fortune, but the ascent must be made step by step.

COMMENTARY Acting thus will lead to the fulfilment of what we will.

6 FOR THE TOP PLACE A night ascent— advantage lies in unremitting persistence.

COMMENTARY But the night ascent will lead to loss, not to wealth.

As all the lines in Lucy's hexagram were changing except the top one, she drew a further hexagram to show the result of following the action recommended in Hexagram 46, the changing solid lines becoming broken and vice versa. This produced:

Looking this up, she found it was Hexagram 17.

HEXAGRAM 17

SUI FOLLOWING, ACCORDING WITH

Component trigrams:

Below: Chen, thunder, movement, to sprout or quicken.

Above: Tui, a body of water, pool, marsh, joy.

TEXT Following. Sublime success! Righteous persistence brings reward— no error!

COMMENTARY ON THE TEXT In this hexagram, the firm comes beneath the yielding; moreover, (the trigrams of) movement and joy are conjoined— hence sublime success, the reward of our persistence and freedom from error. This implies that the whole universe accords with what the times dictate for it. Great indeed is this principle of according with the pulse of time.

SYMBOL This hexagram symbolizes thunder rumbling within a swamp! When darkness falls, the Superior Man goes within and rests peacefully.

Excitedly, when Brian returned from work, she showed him both hexagrams and their commentaries.

"Brian, it's absolutely clear. It foretells success, and recommends going south!"

"Lucy, I don't really believe all that, but it does seem curious that it indicates going south. I suggest that I will apply for the job in Sydney, and you contact your father. Either may not be successful, but if they are both positive then that's what we'll do."

Lucy flung her arms around Brian and kissed him on the cheek.

Over the course of the next few days Brian raised another issue with Lucy.

"Lucy, at some point you will have to go back to Britain, and your former companions on the trip may well be there too. Would you feel safe, knowing that they probably regard you as having let them down in their enterprise?"

Lucy thought about this.

"I don't think Kevin or either of the girls would be a problem. But Davy was different. Although he mostly likes to portray himself as a joker and a fun guy, he can also be very cold, hard and calculating, and I did end up being really scared of him. What are you thinking?"

"I'm wondering if we should let the authorities know in advance that Davy and his companions may try entering the UK in possession of heroin. If they were caught with substantial amounts, it would probably mean custodial sentences."

"Yes, in some ways that would be good. And it would take whatever heroin they had out of circulation. I came to realise, with what happened to Zak, what a horrible, awful, evil trade it is. But getting them put away – especially Davy – would probably only make him angrier and more vengeful when he would be released."

"Yes, there is that. But that would only be the case if he knew that you were instrumental in getting him busted. Perhaps we could do it so that he wouldn't know."

"That sounds good, but what had you in mind?"

"Well, our mutual cousin, Philip Butler, is a lawyer with close contacts in the prosecution service in London. If I telephoned him and told him the position, he might tip off the customs officers and the police to keep an eye out for Davy and his companions as they re-enter the country, to single them out for searching. Then if heroin is found on them, the police will simply charge them and take it from there. I don't see that they need ever know that the police were tipped off, or by whom."

"That seems like a good idea. But Davy is clever. He wanted to hide the heroin firstly in my prosthesis, and then when I stopped being able to use it, in my crutches. I wonder if he'll try something like that."

"I'll tell that to Philip, and he can let the police know the sort of things Davy might do."

Accordingly, Brian telephoned Philip and gave him a brief summary (international phone calls from India to the UK were neither cheap nor very reliable in those days), following this up with a more detailed letter sent by airmail.

Lucy wrote to her father, giving a rough outline of everything that had happened, and asking whether, if Brian managed to get the job he was after in a hospital in Sydney, both she and Brian could come and stay with him – until Brian got his own accommodation, and Lucy found some means of returning to the UK.

Simultaneously Brian submitted his application for a contract with the hospital he had mentioned in Sydney.

Meanwhile, Lucy continued her recovery from her surgery, getting stronger by the day, and following Brian's directions regarding exercise. She also regularly meditated, focussing on her breath, which she found not only to be a calming influence on her, but helped her put into perspective everything that had happened – especially Zak's death. Over the course of eight days she smoked her remaining cigarettes, the last one on her nineteenth birthday, relishing each one, but determined that they would be her last. Once they were finished she did not acquire any more. She also suddenly realised that she hadn't smoked any hashish since before Zak had died – and didn't really miss it or want to get stoned anymore. The one ounce she had left she handed to Brian to dispose of as he saw fit.

She was soon strong enough to be able to go out and see something of the city – sometimes with Brian, when he was off duty, sometimes on her own. She discovered that Bangalore had two distinct parts: the old, Indian part of the city (by far the larger part), which had been the headquarters of Tipu Sultan, the eighteenth-century ruler of southern India, known as the 'Tiger of Mysore', and the 'cantonment', where the British Army and administration, together with their wives and families, had been based. The latter still retained much of its Britishness, although almost all the British residents had departed when India gained independence in 1947, though a sizeable Anglo-Indian population remained, as did many

Tamils (the British had brought Tamil soldiers from Madras, now Chennai, to be stationed in the cantonment in Bangalore. Many had settled, bringing their families with them).

Lucy noted the regional variations in Indian cuisine. In northern India chapattis, naans and parathas were as common a form of carbohydrate as rice, and yoghurt was widely available and used in many dishes. In Goa the Portuguese influence resulted in spicy curries with a wine vinegar base – the famous vindaloo – and coconut, either grated fresh or in the form of coconut milk, was widely used, as was fish (being on the coast). In Bangalore Lucy developed a taste for dosas – crispy rice-flour pancakes, served with a variety of chutneys, or with a spicy potato or vegetable filling.

As everywhere in India, Lucy found that no-one took any particular notice of a young European girl with only one leg, walking on crutches. As always, there were beggars and poor people (though less so in the cantonment area), some of whom had disabilities, so there was nothing particularly startling in this aspect of her appearance.

For Lucy herself, she found it relatively easy to come to terms with now being a hip-level amputee. At no point did she suffer the grief that the loss of her leg at the time of her accident had caused. For the last couple of months prior to her surgery, her stump had been so painful, that having it gone was a relief. On crutches it made little difference to her mobility, and she quite liked the fact that she didn't have a redundant appendage dangling, unsupported. If she was to be on crutches, her new more streamlined body shape was so much the better. Her phantom pains also seemed to have eased considerably. On another level, of course, it took a while to adjust to her new body image, and the fact that there was no part of her left leg remaining. Her 'stump', as she still called it, consisted of soft flesh, in effect her buttock, covering the left underside of her pelvis, with a long scar running across it. It tended to bounce when she hopped, and sometimes she got twitches in it, but otherwise it didn't bother her. She did find, though, that it had become quite sensitive, and she liked to rub and squeeze it, especially if she did have any pain.

As for her self-consciousness in public, Lucy made a conscious decision that, as she was clearly going to have to spend the rest of her life as a one-legged person, she should embrace what she was and not shy away from it or try to hide it. Therefore, in Bangalore, she often chose to wear the thin cotton bloomers that Sita had bought for her and which she had tailored to fit; they were cool and comfortable, and they also showed exactly that all of her leg was missing, which skirts did not (except when she sat down). Moreover, there was no loose fabric flapping around to hamper either her remaining leg or her crutches. She also discovered that, though her underarm crutches took up more room than forearm ones, she really liked them. She felt more supported, by virtue of the saddles pressed into her sides. She decided, in her own mind, that when she went to Australia or returned to Britain, if she was to be a permanent user of crutches she would have both underarm and forearm crutches. The latter were useful for confined spaces and indoors, the former were great for open areas. She again started to actually enjoy going out on her crutches, this time without the possibility of encountering people she had known, or men who wanted to ogle her as an amputee. She especially liked displaying her proficiency and agility on her crutches, which actually astonished and delighted her.

As for the future, for Lucy that was very much an unknown quantity. She couldn't make plans too far ahead. She found comfort in what she remembered of Swami Yogananda's advice, to live in the moment, and for now she took each day as it came. She tended to look upon Brian almost like a brother, a friend she had known since childhood, who was a tower of strength and could be relied upon to provide her with advice, support and guidance through a difficult and uncertain time, and she was very grateful to him. She well knew that any hospital fees she had incurred he had paid, as well as providing her with food and accommodation.

In due course answers were received from both the hospital in Sydney and from Patrick Ryan, Lucy's father. The hospital was prepared to offer Brian a six-month contract as a resident physician in its general medical department, which could be extended by a further six months if all parties agreed. Lucy's father was effusive in suggesting that both she and Brian could come and stay with him and his partner, Ellen, for as long as they liked. Could Lucy let him know when they would be arriving?

The four weeks remaining on Brian's Bangalore contract at the time Lucy was discharged had passed quickly, and he made travel arrangements for the two of them. Lucy was aware that, on top of everything else he had already paid on her behalf, he was paying her travel costs, which were a lot more than her living costs while she had been staying with him, and she felt both guilty and grateful. She tried to raise the issue with him, but he simply smiled and said, "Well, what are friends for?"

Soon it was time for them to leave Bangalore, and indeed India, and head to Australia.

CHAPTER FOURTEEN

Australia – Part One

✦

B rian had two weeks between arrival in Sydney and commencing his job in the hospital. They had received a letter from Lucy's father, which read:

You can both stay with us, and for the first few days we'll show you Sydney (we'll both take a week or two off from our jobs). Then I suggest we drive up to our beach house in Byron Bay, with an overnight stay in Port Macquarie on the way. Byron Bay is a bit of a hippy colony, but it's friendly, the beach is fantastic, and you can relax and enjoy the sea – go surfing every day if you want! Then when we come back to Sydney, Brian can look for accommodation – we might be able to help with that. Lucy, of course, can stay with us as long as she likes.

With love, yours always,

Patrick and Ellen

They travelled by air, and it took five flights to get them from Bangalore to Sydney, the first two with Indian Airlines, the rest with BOAC (which a few weeks later merged with BEA to become British Airways): Bangalore to Madras (now Chennai); Madras to Columbo (Ceylon, now Sri Lanka); Columbo to Singapore; Singapore to Dawin; Darwin to Sydney. They made an overnight stop in Columbo, staying in a hotel, but for the BOAC legs they stayed on the plane and the journey took from lunchtime in Columbo until early the following day in Sydney.

They finally arrived in Sydney at around 7:00 in the morning, utterly exhausted.

They went through passport control, collected their luggage, which Brian put on a trolley, and then cleared customs. Patrick Ryan and his partner, Ellen, met them. Patrick, now in his late forties, and beginning to go grey, was otherwise much as Lucy remembered him except older and slightly bigger around the waist. Ellen was in her late thirties, pretty, with long sun-bleached blonde hair and big brown eyes. She was Australian, but had met Patrick when she was living in England in the 1960s. As Lucy and Brian emerged into the arrivals area Patrick and Ellen stepped forward.

"Oh my god!" Patrick said. "Here's my daughter, all grown up, and pretty as a picture. Lucy, I'm sorry I missed so much of your childhood. And I'm sorry I wasn't around to provide any support after your accident. I'll try and make it up to you." He turned to Brian. "And here's Brian, too. Last time I saw you, you were still a kid." He still had his Dublin accent. Then he introduced Ellen.

Patrick and Ellen led them to their car in the carpark, a big Ford pickup with an open luggage space behind the cabin, which could seat six. Patrick drove, and from the airport, built on the shore of Botany Bay, they headed north through the city centre and over the iconic Sydney Harbour Bridge, getting views of the equally iconic Sydney Opera House.

As they travelled, they all filled in some of their stories. Patrick and Ellen, after they moved to Australia, had acquired jobs – he as a journalist on a national daily newspaper, and she as a producer for one of Australia's television networks. They had obviously done well for themselves. Patrick had given up drinking.

Patrick and Ellen lived in a spacious and comfortable house in the leafy suburbs of Beauty Point, on the north side of Sydney. Once Lucy and Brian were installed, they retired to their guest rooms to catch up on sleep, while Ellen set about making lunch, which she correctly assumed would be a late one. Indeed, for most of the rest of the day, Lucy and Brian relaxed or dozed, on their beds in the guest rooms and later on sun loungers in the garden.

Lucy and Brian stayed with Patrick and Ellen for the next three days, and Patrick drove them around Sydney – into the city centre, to the Opera House, and around some of the shoreline drives, including a visit to Bondi Beach. Patrick was effusive (much more so than Lucy remembered him being when she was a child), and Ellen was straightforward but somewhat outspoken. Both Lucy and Brian privately agreed that, while they were pleasant in small doses, they would not want to stay with them for too long. However, the one thing Lucy most missed – and longed for – was a violin that she could play and practise on. She did, however, keep up her meditation practice, which required no external accoutrements.

After they had been in Sydney for three nights, they all packed into the car and set off northwards along the main coast road, heading for the beach house in Byron Bay.

Patrick had offered some practical advice as they set off.

"Don't go bush unless you know what you're doing, or you're with someone who does. Wallabies and koalas are harmless and look pretty, but brown snakes can be deadly, and funnel web spiders are also to be avoided at all costs. And at the beach keep a lookout for sharks. They don't often come in close, and the lifeguards usually spot them pretty quick. And if you are going to the reef, wear something on your feet – flip-flops will do fine. Coral is very sharp and causes nasty cuts and rashes that can get infected – coral poisoning."

Despite Patrick's dire warnings, the journey was very pleasant and exciting. Both Patrick and Brian had cameras, and on the journey they took quite a few photos. By now Lucy had ceased to be concerned about being stared at, and was largely oblivious to such concerns each time they stopped, which they did for comfort breaks, at a café for refreshments, and for photos when they spotted a koala in a eucalyptus tree and when they saw a group of wallabies grazing, and when they eventually arrived at their overnight hotel in Port Macquarie. Although she still occasionally felt self-conscious, and was aware of one or two people staring at her, it was a minor issue that she ignored, knowing that she had to learn to live with it.

They checked out after breakfast, and continued their journey northward along the coast.

Arriving in Byron Bay in the late afternoon, they stopped at a grocery store and bought some provisions before continuing to Patrick's beach house. The house lay between the road and the beach. It was a wooden construction, roomy enough with two bedrooms, bathroom, kitchen, and living room with a sofa bed, and with a wide veranda overlooking the beach, equipped with table, chairs and sun loungers. Having put their food in the kitchen, and taken their bags to their respective rooms (Brian insisted on Lucy having a bedroom, indicating that he would be fine in the living room on the sofa bed), Lucy and Ellen cooked a meal while Patrick and Brian went for a swim before sunset. Then they all sat on the veranda to eat, and watched the moon rise over the sea, listening to the regular rhythm of the breakers as they crashed and rolled up the beach.

Later, they quickly went to sleep, tired by the two-day journey.

Both Lucy and Brian awakened early, and they watched the sun rise over the ocean, then went down to the beach for a swim before breakfast. There were one or two other people on the beach, some distance away, but Lucy took no notice of them. She had acquired herself a bikini one day when they had gone shopping in Sydney, and now stripped down to it. She knew Brian, as a doctor, had seen her amputation several times during her rehabilitation and stay with him, but even so she felt somewhat self-conscious in front of him in just a bikini. The long scar across her groin, now some two months after her surgery, had faded from a dark red to a paler pink (as time went on it would fade further to a creamy, slightly yellowish colour, lighter than the surrounding flesh). Leaving her crutches and her glasses on a towel well above the surf line, she hopped down the beach, helped by Brian, until she got far enough into the sea to swim.

As in Kavala, Lucy loved the feeling of freedom of movement, supported by the water, with no crutches or mobility aids needed. However, the waves frightened her a bit. They were big Pacific rollers that came foaming in to crash on the beach – great for surfing, but strong enough to easily knock Lucy over when she tried to stand, with only her one leg to balance upon, very different from the calm waters of the Aegean. However, Brian, who was a strong swimmer, stayed close enough to ensure she didn't get into any difficulties.

After their swim they quickly dried off and got dressed, Lucy putting on her glasses and picking up her crutches. They arrived back at the house just as Patrick came out onto the veranda to announce that breakfast was ready.

After breakfast, Brian and Lucy decided to have a look around Byron Bay. Heading out on foot (Lucy on her crutches, wearing one of the cotton skirts Sita had bought her in Bangalore, with a sandal on her foot), they proceeded along Lawson Street and then up Jonson Street. They were about to enter a coffee shop when a voice from across the street hailed them.

"Hey, Lucy! Fancy you being here!"

It was Kevin, and with him was Mandy.

"Oh my god!" muttered Lucy quietly, so only Brian could hear. Out loud she then called back, "Hi, Kevin. Hi, Mandy. What a coincidence!"

Kevin started across the road, Mandy in tow. "Far out! It must be our karma to meet again! We wondered what had happened to you."

Lucy turned to Brian, and mouthed the word, 'Help!' at him. Aloud again, "Brian, this is Kevin and Mandy, friends of mine from my journey to India." Turning to Kevin and Mandy, "This is my friend, Brian."

"Hi, Brian. Cool, happening to meet Lucy here, other side of the world." Kevin grinned. "You guys about to have a coffee? Great. Let's all have one."

Mandy didn't say anything, just grinned rather sheepishly.

So they trooped into the coffee shop, and ordered coffees.

They seated themselves around a table, Kevin opposite Lucy.

"I see you got new crutches, then?" Kevin asked.

"Yes."

"We really wondered what had happened to you, back in Goa. You vanished into thin air. We even thought you might have been so upset by what happened to Zak that you went into the sea and never came out. Especially when your crutches turned up in the flea market."

"Oh?"

"Yeah. Then Davy started banging on about his heroin-smuggling project. He came up with this crackpot scheme. He bought your old crutches in the market, and he was going to get Pete – you remember him? The medical graduate? – to put Jessica's leg in a plaster cast, with heroin inside the cast, and more heroin in the crutches, and then head back to England by bus. He figured the police and customs people wouldn't think to search a girl on crutches with an apparently broken leg. Mandy and I didn't fancy getting involved in that, so we split from them, and we hit the old hippy trail – Calcutta, Rangoon, Bangkok, Bali, and now here. How come you guys are here?"

"My dad lives in Sydney, and he has a beach house here."

"Wow, far out. So what *did* happen to you, Lucy?"

"Like you, I didn't want to be part of Davy's smuggling plans – especially after what happened to Zak. So I split, acquiring some old wooden crutches along the way. I didn't know mine had ended up in the flea market. I was very sick – I had a bad infection in my stump. I knew Brian – who is an old friend and a sort of relative of mine – was working in Bangalore, so I went there. I ended up in hospital – had to have an operation – and then when I recovered and Brian's contract in Bangalore ended, we came here."

Mandy, sitting beside Lucy on her left, glanced at Lucy's lap, and noticed that her skirt was completely flat on the that side – no residual limb left. She gasped.

"Oh my god, Lucy, you had the rest of your leg amputated!"

"Yeah, that was the operation," said Lucy, deeply embarrassed. "I had to, it was too badly infected."

They finished their coffee, then Brian and Lucy stood up, Lucy slipping her crutches under her arms.

"Probably see you around," Brian said, as they left the coffee shop and headed back to the beach house.

Lucy was out of sorts on the way back. Neither she nor Brian said anything until they were almost home.

"Brian, I'm sorry about all that. I never expected to see them here. It gave me a real shock!"

Brian was thoughtful. "It's actually quite good, the way it's happened. But I should let Philip know as soon as possible. If Davy, Jessica and Pete haven't crossed the English Channel yet, the police will know what to look for."

"Yes, I suppose so. And I'm glad that Mandy and Kevin felt the same as me – not wanting to be involved. I've known Mandy for as long as I've known you. It was just the shock of seeing them here. I nearly died! For a moment I thought Davy had sent them and they had tracked me. Of all the places in the whole wide world, and they turn up here!"

"Yeah, it's quite some coincidence. I don't think there's a phone in the house. Of course there's a post office, we walked past it, but the time difference will make phoning difficult. Maybe I should send a telegram."

Arriving back at the house, they told Patrick and Ellen what had happened. Patrick agreed that Brian should send a telegram to Philip. As he was about to drive to Jonson Street to go to the bank and get some shopping, he offered Brian a lift back there.

When they had gone, Ellen turned to Lucy. "So, Lucy. You and Brian aren't an item yet?"

"An item? What do you mean?"

"Boyfriend and girlfriend."

"What? You can't be serious! Brian is like a brother to me. I've known him since I was about four or five years old. He's my cousin's cousin. Anyway, he is my doctor. It would be unethical."

"Not at all. In both the First and Second World Wars many wounded soldiers fell in love with and subsequently married their nurses. It's human nature. Sure, you've known him a long time and you might regard him as a brother, but I'm telling you, he's in love with you!"

"You're not serious. I can't believe that!"

"Oh it's true, all right. I've seen the way he looks at you. He loves you."

This was Lucy's second big shock of the day. She went into her room, lay down on the bed, and thought about it, her thoughts in a whirl. Could it be true? But Brian hadn't said anything to her... But then he was too much of a gentleman to do so. Perhaps it was possible. He was always looking out for her, providing her with support, paying for her medical care, food, clothes and travel tickets.

And how did she feel about him? Yes, she had come to look upon him like a brother, and in that sense she loved him. Could she love him in a different way? Then, of course, there was also the fact that she was disabled. If she and Brian were to be more than friends, how would this impact his life? He was strong, fit and healthy, and had a good career with prospects. Even if he was in love with her, would it be right to burden him with an amputee girlfriend or wife? Brian was a kind and thoughtful man... good-looking, too, if she thought about it, tall and well built, with kind dark eyes and short wavy brown hair. Very different to Zak, of course... It was less than three months since Zak had died. Not that she had been deeply in love with Zak, or at least she hadn't thought so at the time, though she had come to realise that, in many ways, she had loved him, and often thought about him. And how was she to face Brian, when he returned, knowing what Ellen had said?

She tried to meditate, but her thoughts kept coming back to the issue of Brian – his feelings for her, and how she felt about him. He was, after all, the most important and dearest man in her life at present. She suddenly felt that, yes, she could easily fall in love with him. But what if Ellen was wrong? She would make a complete fool of herself, and spoil the sibling-like relationship she currently had with him.

She heard her father and Brian come back into the house, and a buzz of conversation, half heard, drifted through the closed door. She heard Ellen say – loudly enough to know that she was intended to hear, "Lunch will be ready in five minutes."

Lucy got up, gathered her crutches, and, opening the door, entered the living room. Patrick was just heading to the bathroom, Ellen was in the kitchen, and Brian was seated on the sofa bed with a bottle of beer. He gestured for Lucy to sit beside him. Rather reluctantly, she did so.

"I sent Philip a telegram," he said. "It read, if I remember it correctly: *'3 probable smugglers – Davy Wilson, Jessica Ellis, Pete Clark (medic). Jessica with leg cast – heroin inside. Also inside crutches. Let police know.'* So, we've done what we can, and we'll see what happens. Beer?"

"Thanks."

He got her a beer, and sat down again. There was an awkward silence. Then they both started to speak at the same moment.

"After you," said Brian.

"No, you go first," Lucy replied.

At that moment, Ellen opened the kitchen door and called, "Tucker's up. Come and get it."

CHAPTER FIFTEEN

Australia – Part Two

✖

Lunch was not the most comfortable meal for either Brian or Lucy. They hardly spoke. As soon as it was finished, Brian got up and turning to her, said, "Lucy, can we go and talk?"

"Okay." Lucy stood up and slipped her crutches under her arms. "Let's go to the beach."

They went outside, down onto the beach.

"Ellen told me what she said to you," Brian said. "Look, Lucy, how I feel about you is immaterial. Just ignore what Ellen said. Forget about it. Our friendship is more important than getting in a tizz over feelings."

"You mean that what she said is true, but you want to ignore it, and bottle your feelings? Look, Brian, since she told me that, I've been doing a lot of thinking. Up to now, I had thought of you as a friend, almost as the brother I never had. But suddenly I do see that how you felt about me may have been rather different.

"My feelings now are all mixed up, and I'm not sure what way they'll resolve. Of course I love you, as a friend, brother, whatever… And I certainly don't want to jeopardise that. Can I come to love you as a boyfriend, lover, husband…? I don't know. Maybe, but I don't know. In time, I guess I'll know one way or the other.

"At the moment I feel I'm still coming to terms with everything that has happened – with Zak, with my leg, with all my experiences in India. But I don't want to lose you on top of all that. So, if you do love me, in whatever way you do, please give me time. But please, also continue to be with me. I need your support."

"Lucy, of course I will. And all that is fine with me. I wasn't expecting you to fall in love with me, and I love being your friend and your 'brother', regardless of how else I might feel about you."

Lucy smiled, then opened her arms to hug him – letting her crutches fall as she did so. Brian hugged her tight, then bent to pick up her crutches, hiding the tears in his eyes.

They strolled along the beach towards Fisherman's Lookout. Lucy, in spite of herself, almost wished that she wasn't on crutches, so that she might be able to hold Brian's hand as they walked. An easy good humour had been re-established between them, though they both knew that somehow it was slightly different from how it had been.

Returning to the house, they relaxed for the rest of the day, again having a leisurely meal on the veranda and watching the moon rise.

The next day, all four of them went for a swim before breakfast, and later Brian and Lucy again went for a stroll along the beach.

When they got back to the house Patrick met them on the veranda, holding out an envelope to Brian.

"Telegram for you, Brian. It arrived about fifteen minutes ago "

Brian tore open the envelope, and read:

D Wilson, J Ellis, P Clark arrested Dover today late pm. As described. 1.3kg heroin recovered. In custody. Philip Butler.

He showed it to Lucy.

"Oh, wow! They did get busted. I'm a bit sorry for Jessica – she was nice to me, but she shouldn't have gone along with the scheme. But I'm glad Davy got caught."

The next day they set out to return to Sydney, again stopping overnight in Port Macquarie.

Back in Sydney, Brian had ten days before his new contract started, and he knew he had to use it to find accommodation, as he could not realistically go on imposing on the hospitality of Patrick and Ellen. Patrick had contacts in the real estate sector in Sydney, and helped Brian make enquiries about suitable flats for lease. Lucy wanted to go with Brian to view a few of these, and together they found one that was more or less between Patrick and Ellen's home and the hospital where Brian would be working. The rent was reasonable, and while the flat wasn't luxurious, it was adequate – open-plan living room and kitchen (with a small balcony), one medium-size bedroom, one very small bedroom, which would do as an office or study, and a bathroom. Brian duly signed the lease.

Another thing Brian did during this period was take Lucy to one of the foremost musical instrument shops in Sydney, and bought her a very nice violin.

"You shouldn't have," said Lucy. "I haven't come to any decision yet about us."

"It's a belated birthday present," he told her. "No strings – except, of course, those on the violin!"

Lucy laughed, and thanked him.

A couple of days later, Brian moved into his flat. With her father and stepmother both back at work, Lucy had their house to herself for considerable periods over the next few weeks. She spent her time practising her new violin, meditating, cooking, and wondering what she should do. She really liked Brian, but she wasn't sure she was in love with him. But then, she hadn't been in love with Zak, either – at least not until he was dead. She missed him, and the memories of how he had died, and the subsequent callousness of Davy haunted her. She was very thankful for the meditation that Swami Yogananda had taught her, as it enabled her to put these feelings into some sort of perspective. She thought of asking the I Ching for guidance, but decided that to do so would be to cop out of what had to be her own decision. And while she didn't feel she was ready yet to commit to Brian, she didn't want to be parted from him either. While Patrick had told her she could stay as long as she liked, and he was still her father, she really didn't want to impose on him and Ellen indefinitely. She had no source of income, so she couldn't just move out and stay in Sydney. If she returned to the UK she would be parting – at least for several months – from Brian.

During this period, having asked Patrick about dentists, and having been referred by him to his own, she went and got her braces adjusted as they were now well overdue for this.

Another thing she did – with Brian – was to attend a concert in the Sydney Opera House, which they both enjoyed immensely.

Now totally reliant on crutches to get around, for the most part Lucy encountered helpfulness and smiles whenever she was out and about – people held doors open for her, offered her seats on public transport, and helped her carry a tray of food if she was in a self-serve café. However, she once again occasionally encountered a few men who either ogled her or tried to follow her. In his capacity as a doctor, she asked Brian about this one day, when they were able to meet for a meal in a restaurant. Brian was shocked, and initially blushed and stammered something, then said, "Yes, there are men who are sexually attracted to women with disabilities. It is a recognised phenomenon. If they display behaviour that is unacceptable, that is no excuse, and they should be dealt with appropriately.

"Lucy, if you have been bothered by people like this, you need to go out with someone you know, or stay in a safe area where there are other people about. Don't go out alone in areas you don't know, and don't go out alone after dark."

He then changed the subject, asking her if she had thought about getting fitted for a hip-level prosthesis.

"No, I haven't thought about it. I don't know how I would go about it. There isn't a National Health Service here, and I don't have health insurance. In any case, as I understand it, most people with my level of amputation find it too difficult to wear a prosthesis, and usually prefer to just use crutches."

"Yes, that is true, but not that many hip-level amputees are young and otherwise healthy. The technology in prosthetics has advanced a lot in the last twenty years, and it continues to advance, so do think about it. As for health insurance, you could join a scheme – your father could probably put you on his policy without too much bother."

Later, back in her room at Patrick and Ellen's house, Lucy went over the discussion in her mind. She had a sudden insight, what is termed a 'lightbulb moment' – that Brian himself was one of these people who were attracted to amputees. She almost felt sick at the realisation. There and then she decided that she must return to England as soon as possible. Much as she had come to rely on Brian, even to love him, how could she possibly stay here and continue even a close friendship with him, knowing what she now knew?

At breakfast the next morning, Lucy told her father and Ellen that she had decided to return to the UK as soon as possible.

"The only problem is, I don't have enough money for the fare. I suppose I could phone Mum and ask her, but I'm not sure she wouldn't be under pressure to come up with that much money."

Patrick immediately responded, "Lucy, I'm your father. I'll pay your fare if that's what you've decided. I'm just disappointed that you want to leave so soon, just as we were getting to know each other again."

"Oh, Dad. It's not that I haven't enjoyed being here with you, or that I'm tired of your company. But, when I left for India, I put my life on hold back there, and it's still on hold. I want to go to university or music college, and I want to see Mum. My life is there, not here – much as I've loved being here. Anyway, you and Ellen can't have me imposing on you indefinitely. And thank you, I would be so eternally grateful if you could pay my fare."

Later, when Ellen managed to catch Lucy alone, she looked at her, raised her eyebrows and asked the one crucial question: "Brian?"

"It's not going to work out, Ellen. And I've decided that I have to leave as soon as possible."

Two days later, Lucy was on a flight to London.

Brian received a letter she had left for him:

Dear Brian,

Sorry, but it isn't going to work. I've decided it's best I return immediately to the UK.

Thank you for all you have done for me. I don't think I can ever repay you.

Lucy

CHAPTER SIXTEEN

Picking Up the Pieces

L ucy arrived at her mother's house exhausted – physically from the journey, and mentally from the anguish she had been going through over Brian. Had she been correct in her assumption of his attraction? She was fairly certain she was. Had she been correct in breaking off with him a friendship that had never – from her side – progressed into anything more? This was more problematic. She knew Brian well enough to know that he would be deeply upset. Should she care – if he was one of *them*? She didn't know.

Lucy didn't want to discuss it with anyone, least of all her mother. Indeed she told Helen only basic factual information about the entire trip, not going into details on Davy's heroin-smuggling proposals (Helen was aware that he and Jessica plus another man had been arrested), saying nothing about Swami Yogananda and Lakshmi, and nothing about Brian's feelings for her. In order to take her mind off it all, she busied herself in other things – applying to universities, practising on her two violins (she had kept the one Brian had given her) and on the piano, which she hadn't played for almost a year (the last keyboard instrument she played was the electronic keyboard with the band, before the trip to India), and meditating, from which she continued to derive a degree of comfort and perspective.

Helen, for her part, knew Lucy well enough not to try and pry too deeply into what had obviously been a tumultuous and at times traumatic few months. She learned enough from Lucy about Zak's addiction and death, and about her osteomyelitis and the revision of her amputation to a hip disarticulation (which Lucy could not very well hide from her anyway), and formed her own conclusions as to what had passed between Lucy and Brian, first in India and then in Australia. Overall she was glad to have her daughter back, if not exactly in one piece, at least alive.

As she settled back to life in Sussex, without Zak or Brian, Lucy decided to do three things.

Firstly, she acquired herself a new pair of forearm crutches. While she liked the axillary crutches she had been given by the hospital in Bangalore, especially when she was in outdoor spaces, she found them to be rather awkward and cumbersome in confined spaces inside buildings, and in any case she felt it probably best to have more than one pair of crutches – especially if she was going to be constantly and permanently reliant on them.

This brought up her second decision: she decided that she *would* seek getting fitted for a new hip-level prosthesis. She at least wanted to try and get back to some form of two-legged life, even if it was on a part-time basis. This decision was based on two principal factors: if she didn't try a new prosthesis she would always wonder whether she would have been able to use one, and for practical purposes at university or if she was performing it might be preferable to appear on two legs if she possibly could. For all other times she was now perfectly content to remain one-legged, using crutches. If nothing else, her journeying had taught her that it was irrelevant whether people stared, or thought she was an object of pity. She no longer pitied herself, and never would. On the contrary, she was actually proud of herself for how she had withstood all life had thrown at her, and regarded her amputation and scars as badges of honour for battles she had gone through and prevailed.

Thirdly, she decided to go and visit Zak's parents. She felt she owed that much to his memory.

The first two were initiated by making an appointment and visiting her GP. She told him about the trip to India, that her stump had become infected, and that she ended up in hospital and had to have a revision, leaving her as a hip-level amputee. She said she would like a pair of underarm crutches, and he immediately wrote her a prescription for these, so she had only to pay a token sum for them. She also asked to be referred to the limb-fitting centre as soon as possible, so that she could see if it would be possible for her to be fitted with – and learn to walk upon – a hip-level prosthesis, preferably before she commenced university in the autumn of 1974. Her GP readily agreed to make the referral.

Lucy then spent some time drafting and redrafting a letter to Zak's parents. The final version, which she posted to them with her address and phone number at the top, read:

Dear Mr and Mrs Goldberg,

My name is Lucy Ryan. You may remember me from my visits to the garage at your house as part of the band that Zak established. As I am sure you are aware, I also became Zak's girlfriend, and lived with him for the best part of two years (less a few months when I was recovering from a motorbike accident in which, as you may be aware, I lost a leg).

I was also part of the group that travelled to India in Zak's old VW campervan, and was with him throughout that journey, including when he died.

I would like to express my sincere condolences to you on the loss of your son. While Zak undoubtedly had addiction issues, which my best efforts were unfortunately unable to resolve, and which ultimately led to his death, I may say that he was a kind and gentle soul, who always treated me with affection, dignity and respect, and I miss him greatly.

While I have no wish to impose myself upon you if you do not wish to see me, I would dearly love to be able to come and talk to you about Zak, to give you more information regarding where and how he died, and maybe share memories of him that will help us all, and also be a fitting tribute to him.

Yours sincerely,

Lucy Ryan

Two days later, she got a phone call.

"Hello, is that Lucy? It's Ruth Goldberg here. We got your letter, and I want to thank you for it. It was very touching. My husband Ben and I would love to meet with you. Would you be able to come over to our house – you know where it is – for tea on Saturday, say about 4 o'clock?"

Because she had no transport of her own and didn't want to involve her mother, Lucy got a taxi to Zak's parents' house on that Saturday afternoon, arriving just after 4 o'clock.

Ruth Goldberg met Lucy at the door, and brought her into a big living room with mullioned windows, a Tudor-arch fireplace, oak-beamed ceiling, and chintz armchairs and sofas. Ben Goldberg stood up to greet Lucy, and waved her to a chair. Ben was of medium height, dark-haired going grey, and an older version of Zak, minus beard and long hair. Ruth was also dark-haired, slightly plump, with a round open face on which, despite her welcoming smile, grief was evident.

Lucy sat, leaning her new forearm crutches against the arm of her chair.

Ruth pulled over a hostess trolley on which sat teapot, milk and sugar, cups, saucers and plates, and an array of cakes and sandwiches. She poured a cup of tea, placing it on a side table beside Lucy's chair.

"Milk and sugar?"

"Yes, please, milk and one spoonful."

"And do have something to eat." Ruth brought the trolley within Lucy's reach. Lucy took a sandwich, which turned out to be cream cheese and cucumber, and a slice of sponge cake. Ruth poured tea for herself and Ben.

"So, dear, you wanted to tell us about Isaac."

For just a moment Lucy wondered who they meant, then realised that, of course, this had been Zak's real name, though everyone always called him 'Zak' – except, it seemed, his parents.

"We didn't get on," Ben said rather gruffly. "Never understood why he behaved as he did, getting into drugs and all that rock music, and looking like some scruff who had never met a barber in his life!"

"Now, Ben," Ruth remonstrated. "Lucy didn't come here to be lectured."

"Yes, well, sorry. But I thought you should know."

"Actually, I did know," said Lucy. "Zak told me that you didn't altogether see eye to eye with him, though he always expressed love and admiration for you. But, like many young people these days, he had different values and interests from your generation. He loved music – of lots of different genres – I heard him play classical records as well as rock. He felt there were more important values than money or social standing.

"I am not trying to defend his use of heroin. Far from it. I hated to see him using it. I think he started using it as an experiment, as a different means of getting high rather than cannabis or LSD. Though I'm not into it now, when I lived with him, I used to regularly smoke cannabis – I found its effects to be very pleasant, and after my accident I also found it helped with pain relief. Of course, it was probably also partly responsible for my accident in the first place, as I was rather stoned at the time, which isn't a good thing to be when riding a motorbike, though not as dramatic as being drunk. So, anyway, I know why Zak got into that, in the first place. He also introduced me to LSD, which I took twice. The first time was probably the most magical and wonderful experience I've ever had, but the second was absolute hell, and I immediately decided never to try it again.

"But, as I said in my letter to you, I always found Zak to be a gentleman, kind and thoughtful, and I think that was very much the result of how you brought him up."

Ruth brushed a tear from her face, and then asked Lucy questions about the trip to India, where they had been, what they had done. Lucy gently related the story, up to the point they arrived in Goa.

"That was where everything finally fell apart. It should have been wonderful. Goa is a tropical paradise – gorgeous beaches fringed with palm trees, little thatched beach houses, a bustling local market, good food... But, Zak..." Here, Lucy herself had to pause and wipe away a tear. "Zak injected himself with a shot of heroin that mustn't have been pure. He became delirious, then had shivering fits before sinking into a coma. There was another hippy there who had studied medicine, and he came and sat with Zak as well, until the end came.

"I'm sorry, I don't know what they did after he died. It's customary in India to have the funeral within a day, but I couldn't face it. I assume he was buried – the Hindus cremate their dead, but in Goa there are many Catholics, plus the hippies, so he was probably buried... I'm so sorry..."

Here Lucy broke into fresh sobs. Ruth comforted her.

"Thank you, dear. It's okay. Thank you so much for telling us."

Lucy dried her eyes. "There is one more thing," she said. "The other members of the band. I know two of them went on to Australia – Kevin and Mandy – you probably remember them. But Davy was different. I didn't really like him. He liked to joke around, but at the same time there was a very hard side to him. He came up with a scheme to smuggle heroin back here from India, even after what happened to Zak. And he wanted my help. I couldn't do it, so I left. But I learned that he planned to then use his girlfriend Jessica to bring the drugs in. A friend of mine passed the information on to the authorities so they were alerted and caught Davy and Jessica, along with the hippy I told you about who had studied medicine, when they crossed the Channel. I don't know if the trial has taken place yet, but I imagine they'll be spending a few years in jail."

Both Ben and Ruth thanked Lucy for this information. Ruth then said to her, "Lucy, I think we may have some things of yours. When we were advised by the authorities that Isaac had died in India, we went and cleared out his flat, and settled up with the landlord. Some of the things we found in the flat must be yours – come and see."

Lucy stood and, slipping her arms into the cuffs of her new crutches, followed Ruth out of the living room, across the hall and down a passage to what was obviously a storeroom-cum-utility-room. On one side was a long unit with a worktop and sink, cupboards above, more cupboards and a washing machine and dryer below. On the worktop were two large cardboard boxes, in which Lucy found all the things she had left in Zak's flat – a winter coat and gloves, shoes, skirts, jeans, cardigans, kaftans and blouses, underwear, nightwear, toiletries and manicure items, piles of sheet music, old notebooks, her study books from doing her 'O' and 'A' levels, and a small framed photograph of Barney.

"Wow! I had forgotten I had half this stuff," Lucy exclaimed. "Thank you. I'm not sure how I'll get it home, though."

"Don't worry about that. I know you came in a taxi – I saw it turning out of the drive when I opened the door. I'll get Ben to put these boxes in my car and I'll drive you home.

"There are some books Isaac left, as well. I was going to give them to charity, but if there are any you would like, please help yourself." Ruth opened a wall-cupboard door, displaying a row of books, many of which Lucy recognised.

"Thank you very much. I'd like this one, and this…" She picked out *The Prophet*, and *Jonathan Livingstone Seagull*, and put them into one of the boxes with her own things.

Ben duly put the boxes into the back of their car, and Ruth got into the driver's seat. Ben shook Lucy's hand, and said, "I'm sorry I was so gruff with you at the start. Thank you for coming. You would have made me a fine daughter-in-law."

In the car on the way to Helen's house, Ruth opened the conversation.

"You'll have to excuse Ben. He doesn't really understand the values young people have in this country now. Although he and I were both born in England, and consider ourselves English, both Ben's parents and mine were Jews who came to Britain in the first decade of this century, before the First World War, from Eastern Europe, to escape the pogroms there. We both had various relatives that ended up in the gas chambers during the last war. Ben is of a mind to think that aggression must be countered with aggression. Isaac was born after the war, and was always attracted by pacifist ideas and ideals, reinforced by that awful war in Vietnam that America is involved in. His sympathies were always with the draft dodgers, totally opposed to Ben's views."

"I understand, Mrs Goldberg, and what happened to your relatives in the war is unspeakably awful. But I think Zak was right, certainly as far as Vietnam is concerned. America has been fighting there for so many years, and got nowhere, and so many lives have been lost. So much waste."

"I know," Ruth replied. "I think even Ben is starting to see that that particular war has been a spectacular failure. But he and Isaac disagreed over Israel too. Isaac always said the Palestinian Arabs had just as much right to be there as the Jews. That was a hard one for Ben to take in, after what happened in the Holocaust."

"Yes. It's difficult. All one can do is imagine what it is like to be on one side, and then on the other. There is no absolute right or wrong answer."

"You're very wise for one so young. But then you have been through more in your short life than a lot of people go through in their entire lifetime." She briefly glanced down at Lucy's lap, where her skirt curved over her right leg, and lay flat on the seat on the other side of it. "Isaac's sister, Rebecca, whom I don't think you have met, was always trying to get her father and her brother to see each other's point of view, but never really succeeded. You should meet her some time, I think you'd get on. But she lives up in Manchester, so we don't often see her."

They arrived at Helen's house. Helen came out and she and Ruth carried the two boxes of Lucy's things in, and set them in the hall. Then Ruth thanked Lucy again for going to see them, and she thanked Ruth for listening, and for the tea, and for storing and giving her back her things.

"She seems to be a nice person," Helen remarked, as Ruth drove away.

"Yes, she is," said Lucy. "And despite all his faults, her son was too, although I know you were always suspicious of him."

"Well, he was just so different to anyone I had imagined you ever going out with. I'm sorry, Lucy, if I was wrong about him."

"Thanks, Mum. And you weren't entirely wrong. He was addicted to heroin, and it's not a nice thing to witness. But still, he was a nice guy, and he shouldn't have died the way he did.

"Anyway. I had better sort out all this stuff that I had left in his flat."

A couple of weeks later, Lucy went for her first appointment as a hip-level amputee at the orthopaedic hospital's limb-fitting centre. The chief prosthetist himself came and examined Lucy, and outlined to her what she could expect.

"A hip-disarticulation prosthesis is a lot more complex and difficult than a transfemoral one," he said. "Instead of having lost two major joints, you have lost three. And as there is no residual limb to which to fit the prosthesis, we have to construct a socket that encases your pelvis. The basic process of fitting is similar to what you have previously experienced, but the resultant prosthesis is significantly different, and walking with it presents different and more difficult challenges.

"We will start by casting you, as we did for your transfemoral prosthesis. Then we make a trial socket, and will make whatever adjustments are needed until that is right. Then we attach the leg part, with a joint at the front of the socket to function as your hip.

"Learning to walk with it will present you with the most challenging part of the process, and not everyone finds it cost effective in terms of effort and comfort and mobility. But, if you want to succeed and are prepared to persevere, it can provide a significant benefit to you."

Lucy then had to wait in the waiting room for the plaster-cast technicians to cast her. There were various people in the waiting room including another leg amputee, a woman in her mid-twenties, with her right leg amputated at about the same level as Lucy's initial amputation, who got into conversation with her. It transpired that her name was Morag, she was Scottish, and her leg had been amputated when she was twelve years old due to osteosarcoma, an aggressive bone cancer. She was being fitted for a new prosthesis, her fifth in fourteen years.

"Aye, well, we have to make the most of what we have, and what we haven't!" Morag said with a laugh. "In some ways it has its benefits."

"Do you think so?" Lucy asked, somewhat bemused.

"Oh, aye! A one-legged lassie can have a whale of a time if she plays her cards right. Seats offered, doors held open, special parking spaces, and lads who want to wait on you hand and foot. Sure, there's the downsides, but why focus on them? I know, for me, I almost lost my life, and I'm very grateful for every day I have, so I want to make the most of it, in every way I can. And if having one leg less makes the rest of me more special, then so much the better." Morag smiled and winked.

"Do you mean that you don't mind men who think an amputee girl is sexy just because they're an amputee?" Lucy asked.

"Not at all. Of course, it depends on the man. Some are creeps. But most are nice guys, and if they like me for what I am, why should I mind. Anyway, what's the choice? Wait for some man who thinks I would be gorgeous if it wasn't for the missing leg? But that's going to put him off. So if some man thinks I'm gorgeous anyway, and even more gorgeous *with* a missing leg, I'm all for it!"

For Lucy, this was a whole new perspective. She had assumed that any man finding a woman with an amputation attractive was at best warped, if not an outright pervert.

"So you don't consider them all to be perverts?"

"Not at all. A few might be, but by and large they're the exception. You wear glasses – would you consider a man to be a pervert if he said he thought you especially attractive with your glasses on? Or if some man said he loved your chestnut hair? So if some man thinks a girl with one leg is attractive, so long as that's not the only reason he likes her, what's wrong with it?"

"No, I suppose you're right," Lucy said, thoughtfully.

At this moment she was summoned to be casted. The process was similar to what she had been through before, except this time the stockinette, the plastic cling wrap, and the plaster-of-Paris bandages were wrapped around her legless hip and up over the crest of her pelvis and round her waist. She had to press down on a hanging sling under her pelvis on the amputated side as the plaster set, so that the right shape would be obtained. Once it did, the cast was cut off and would be used to create a mould of her amputation and waist on which the socket would be formed.

That was it for the first appointment. Over the next eight weeks Lucy had several appointments, tried test sockets and test legs, was fitted with her prosthesis, and practised walking with it. The socket was effectively a plastic bucket or cup that fitted over her pelvis on the amputated side, with a broad semi-stiff belt that went around her waist, tightened with two straps at the front. A steel joint was attached to the front of the socket and fixed to the top of the usual pylon, with knee and foot as previously. Behind the hip hinge was a small strut that, when the leg was pushed slightly backwards relative to the socket, released the knee, allowing it to flex. The entire leg had to be controlled by the way Lucy swung her pelvis forward to take a step, and it proved not only difficult and very tiring, but caused her back to ache unmercifully after doing it a lot. Although it came with the usual cosmesis (foam cover to look like a leg), she decided that it was more practical without this, and when she got the leg home she took it off. This time she had no need of a secret compartment within it.

Several times she met Morag, both at the limb-fitting centre and socially for coffee. She had never previously met another leg amputee in her approximate age group with whom she could compare notes or from whom she could glean support and tips on living successfully as an amputee. Morag's view on men who found female amputees attractive came as a revelation to Lucy, and she thought deeply about it. She began to wonder if she had done the right thing in suddenly splitting up with Brian. She did consider writing to him, but then felt that, having effectively burnt her bridges, it was probably best not open old wounds.

Morag introduced Lucy to her boyfriend, Martin, and the three of them went for a walk along the seafront before having a coffee together. On this occasion both Lucy and Morag were sans prostheses, on crutches, and Martin laughed and said how he felt the luckiest man alive to be with two such beautiful one-legged women.

Lucy liked him, and for the first time felt that a man who admired her, not only for herself but also because she was an amputee, was not some sort of weirdo. Of course this was helped by the fact that she knew it was Morag he most admired, so she felt completely safe. She asked him what it was about amputee girls that attracted him.

"I'm not really sure," he replied. "Partly, I suppose, it's because anyone who is otherwise beautiful, but has had to go through what you girls have gone through, has an added depth to their character, and an inner strength that is incredibly attractive. Physical beauty is so much to the fore these days in everything a woman is supposed to be in attracting a man, but so often very beautiful woman tend to be so very shallow. Then there is beauty in the graceful way a woman moves on her crutches, when she has been an amputee for some time. There are other, more intimate reasons, too…" He looked at Morag and smiled.

Morag laughed. "Easy access, uniquely intimate positions, unusual erogenous zones…"

Martin went scarlet, nearly choked on his coffee, and quickly changed the subject.

Lucy also met again with Ruth Goldberg, who told her that Zak had left the master tapes of the recordings the band had made in the garage-cum-studio. As she, Ruth, didn't know what to do with them, Davy was in prison, and Kevin and Mandy were probably still in Australia or the Far East, she suggested that Lucy might take them. Lucy told her to hold onto them, and she would make enquiries as to what might be the best thing to do with them. She subsequently made a few desultory enquiries, but didn't come to any conclusions regarding the tapes, which at that time were left with the Goldbergs.

During this period Lucy took a series of driving lessons with an instructor who taught disabled drivers, using a car with automatic transmission (as the car had no clutch, the fact that Lucy didn't have a left leg made no difference to her ability to drive an automatic). She had, of course, her motorbike licence, which was now invalid as it was issued before she lost her leg, but the rules of the road remained the same. Of course, she was nervous to begin with, as her experience on the motorbike had resulted in disaster, but as the lessons progressed she gradually gained in confidence. Her mother, with some trepidation, agreed to buy her a second-hand automatic transmission car if she passed her test, which she did in early September.

Over several weeks Lucy slowly got the hang of using her new prosthesis. She found that she could only wear it for relatively limited periods of time, maybe up to four or five hours maximum, before it became too uncomfortable. It did have many drawbacks – it was heavy, sweaty, awkward. She could only walk relatively slowly on it (much slower than on her crutches) with a rather ungainly limp, if she had to bend over it pressed uncomfortably into her tummy, and it aggravated the sensation if she needed to pee by tending to press on her bladder. She also disliked the fact that she had to take it off every time she went to a toilet. Depending on whether she was wearing jeans or a skirt, this involved taking extra time and space, and while it wasn't too bad at home, public toilets were not always accommodating to these needs.

Lucy also liked occasionally to wear a high heel, which she could only do on crutches (adjusting the crutches to allow for the extra height). On her prosthesis, she could only wear flat shoes.

To keep herself in shape she took up swimming. She had left her bikini in Australia, and in any case was reluctant to go to a public swimming pool wearing a bikini (the beach in Byron Bay had been largely deserted), so she bought herself a one-piece swimming costume cut low around the legs, allowing her to sew up the left leg-hole so her stump (she still called it that, though there was no leg left) would be covered. Although one or two people stared to begin with, most people took no notice of the pretty amputee girl at the swimming pool, and she again found how enjoyable it was to be supported by the water and able to move freely without need for any external aids. She quickly became a strong and competent swimmer.

Lucy wrote to Lakshmi in Goa, outlining to her what had happened since she boarded the train to leave Goa in January, including her treatment in hospital and the revision of her amputation, her recovery and visit to Australia to see her father, what had happened with Davy, Jessica and Pete, and a sketchy outline of her friendship with Brian (but omitting details of Brian being in love with her or of her reaction to realising he was attracted to amputees). She once again thanked Lakshmi for her assistance, and asked her to thank Swami Yogananda for his, and for teaching her his meditation. A few weeks later she received a reply:

Dear Lucy

Salutations! I received your kind and most interesting letter, and am most gratified that you arrived in Bangalore, received all necessary treatment, and are alive and well in England, after adventure in Australia.

I was sorry to hear about use to which your old crutches were put, and would not have allowed them to go to market if I had known. But, as law has caught those responsible for bad usage, no harm done.

Swami Yogananda sends you his blessings.

Your sister in spirit

Lakshmi

She was contacted by her cousin, Philip Butler, who told her that Davy had been sentenced to five years in prison, Pete to three years, and Jessica to eighteen months (although she was the carrier of the drugs, she had co-operated fully with the police, and therefore received a lighter sentence). Pete, although he had never registered as a doctor, was debarred from registering.

Towards the end of the summer Lucy had her orthodontic braces adjusted again, and was advised that by the end of the year they could be removed.

Throughout this period, as well as her prosthetic appointments and practice wearing the leg, Lucy assiduously practised her violin and piano playing and her meditation, and she thought a lot about Brian and about what Morag and Martin had said to her. She had also applied to several universities and music colleges, and accepted an offer from one to do a combined music and education degree.

CHAPTER SEVENTEEN

Lucy at University

✠

L ucy wanted a career that was steady, stable and rewarding, but definitely incorporating music. However, she didn't think that a career as a performing musician as such would be suitable for someone with her disability. She certainly couldn't envision herself as a concert violinist, always on tour, living in hotels, nor did she especially want the role or lifestyle of an orchestral player. Therefore, she didn't apply to any of the specialist conservatoires (like the Royal College of Music, the Royal Academy of Music, or the Royal Northern College of Music). The solution that she had decided upon was that she wanted to be a teacher, specialising in music, but preferably in primary education as she didn't think she would be able to cope with teenagers. Therefore she wanted to do a joint honours degree, combining bachelor's degrees in arts, education and music.

Of the various universities she contacted, one in particular seemed promising, neither too far nor too close to her home in Sussex, and she accepted the offer of a place. At that time university education, although not free, was largely covered for the vast majority of students by student grants, so there wasn't a big financial commitment required.

Although it had its ups and downs, Lucy enjoyed university life. She had regained sufficient self-confidence to engage in the social scene (carefully avoiding anything to do with drugs, and though pubs were often on her agenda she never drank to excess). She engaged in quite a lot of extra-mural musical activity, including joining a student string quartet as second violin, with three other music students, which she really enjoyed. As well as continuing with swimming, she also took up hatha yoga. She found a yoga teacher who was able to adapt those few of the poses and exercises that Lucy found difficult with one leg. To her regular yoga practice, she added half an hour of her meditation, as the two naturally complemented each other.

Lucy settled into university life, going to lectures, socialising, and generally becoming more comfortable with herself as an amputee – both on her prosthesis (initially as much of the time as she could do so) and on her crutches (when her prosthesis became too uncomfortable, and always in her room). She made a number of friends, including her roommate, Lizzie, who was doing a BA. High-energy, scatty, always friendly, welcoming and with a big smile on her face, Lizzie was small and wiry with a mass of dark curly hair. She and Lucy instantly hit it off, and she helped Lucy with the occasional difficulties she had because of her amputation, such as ensuring that she had a shower seat available in the bathroom, or carrying her lunch tray in the canteen when she was on her crutches. Lizzie had a quick succession of boyfriends, none of them very serious, and she confided in Lucy that back in Harrogate, where she came from, she had a childhood sweetheart that she was madly in love with – though she was not absolutely certain he was equally committed.

Lucy travelled back to Sussex for the holidays at Christmas and Easter. During the Christmas holidays she went to her dentist and had her braces removed. For a day or two it felt really strange to be without them, but she was pleased with the effect that they had produced on her smile – she now had perfectly even teeth!

Back at university Lucy dated a few boys, but none very seriously. She had no desire to get heavily involved with anyone, let alone intimate, and she still felt very shy about showing her body – with Zak, immediately after her amputation it had initially only been when cannabis had effectively removed her self-consciousness and her inhibitions. Of course, Lucy had desires, and some of the boys were gorgeous, but she wasn't ready, and she was also thinking about both Zak and Brian. She felt that casual sex was maybe something for able-bodied girls, but it wasn't for her. Lucy's dates often wanted things to progress beyond pub visits, cinema outings or restaurant meals, and this confirmed for her that, firstly, having only one leg did not mean that all men were put off – far from it, and secondly, that as outlined by her friend Morag, guys who were attracted to her for reasons that included her one-leggedness could be nice and could be gentlemen. She supposed that she may have broken a few hearts by turning them down (although she wasn't either so vain or so empathetic to their emotions as to really realise this at the time).

The first year at university seemed to pass in a flash. Lucy returned to Sussex for Christmas, Easter and the summer, and soon she was back in university for her second year. Lucy and Lizzie had decided to rent a room in a shared house that was mostly occupied by students, and they quickly settled in. Lizzie was an excellent cook, so although they frequently ate out or availed of the numerous good takeaway food outlets, they never went for lack of good food.

Lucy was now twenty, and it was nearly four years since her initial amputation. As time went on, she became less and less self-conscious about being one-legged, and consequently wore her prothesis less frequently. She always found much greater comfort and greater mobility on crutches; their only real drawback was that her hands were occupied and carrying things was awkward, but she had long since become an expert at using shoulder bags and small backpacks. She also developed a good deal of strength in her arms and shoulders, and in her remaining leg, not only from using crutches but also from swimming and yoga. The ache in her shoulders from being on crutches was of considerably less discomfort than the backache from walking around on the prosthesis. She altered two pairs of jeans by cutting off the left leg of each and sewing them closed so they snugly fitted over her stump, without need to fold up the empty trouser leg, just as she had done in Bangalore with jeans, pyjamas and cotton bloomers.

Lucy still had bouts of phantom limb pain, but they had greatly diminished from the almost constant intensity that she had experienced in the weeks after her initial amputation. They seemed to be affected by changes in the weather, and her monthly cycle, and tended to occur most when these coincided. She did, however, still have frequent sensations in her missing leg – tingling in the foot and toes, and a feeling that her leg was icy cold, even when all the rest of her was hot (even when she was lying in a hot bath!). While it was disconcerting, Lucy had learned to live with it, and largely managed to ignore it. Exercise (swimming, yoga, and generally getting around on her crutches) always helped, as did her meditation, warm baths, and regular sleep.

By this stage all the students who knew Lucy were well aware that she had one leg, and invariably helped her when needed – holding doors open, or carrying breakfast, lunch or dinner trays in cafés and canteens. She realised that it didn't matter if some people (those who didn't know her) stared, or made patronising or pitying comments; as far as she was concerned that was their problem, not hers. Of course, realising this and fully accepting it were two different things. There were occasional incidents when someone's cutting remark or intrusive question infuriated her or reduced her to tears. One memorable occasion was in a pub one night, when Lucy was with Lizzie and a group of friends. Towards the end of the evening, she had just been to the toilet, and a very drunk male student that she didn't know watched her crutch back to her friends. He then came over towards their table, and in a loud voice that everyone in their vicinity could hear, said, "Oh God! Things must be bad! The university must be trying to fill its quotas, or something. It's bad enough they let girls in, but now I see they're letting deformed cripples in as students!"

Fortunately some of the people Lucy was with included several strong men, and they quickly escorted this moron out (with the assistance of one of the bar staff who had also heard), but of course Lucy was absolutely mortified, reduced to tears, and very angry. Lizzie and the others had to calm her down, comfort her and help her back to her room.

This was by far the worst of these incidents, which were rare. People with views like that student were very much in the minority, and for the most part Lucy didn't regret mostly using crutches rather than her prosthesis, which usually sat in a cupboard in her room unless she was performing with the string quartet (she always wore it for concerts).

At the other end of the spectrum from people like that student, less immediately distressing but perhaps scarier, were those – mostly men – who found her disability sexy and alluring but without primarily liking her as a person. Lucy became aware, first, of one male student, a few years older than her, who seemed to make a point of appearing at all the social gatherings, pubs, cinemas, and so on that she went to, and she became aware that he spent a lot of time watching her. Then she received anonymous letters, the first of which read:

Hello Lucy,

You don't know me, but I have seen you about, and I think you are very beautiful. The way you move on your crutches is incredibly sexy. I would love to see and feel your stump.

If you would like to meet with me, I'll be in the bar at ___ Inn tomorrow at 7.00pm. I'll have a red rose in my buttonhole.

I hope you'll come.

An admirer

Needless to say, Lucy avoided going anywhere near the suggested rendezvous. She told Lizzie, and thought of going to speak to the university bursar, but decided not to bother. Over the next few months she got two further letters of a similar nature, but ignored those too.

There was also a young man who attended some of the same classes and lectures that Lucy went to, who was more direct, open and friendly. He approached Lucy one day, and, without being patronising, told her he thought it was great that she was at university, that he admired the way she got on with her life in spite of having only one leg, and asked if they could become friends. Lucy didn't reject him outright, and without agreeing overtly to become his friend, did nod to him and say, "Hi," each time they saw each other, and even went and had coffee with him. He reminded Lucy of Morag's boyfriend, Martin. He was quite sweet, and a nice person, but she wasn't in the market at that stage for any relationship and didn't encourage too close a friendship.

Lucy remembered a compelling yet rather depressing psychological thriller that she had recently read, *The Walking Stick* by Winston Graham. The protagonist was a young woman who had become disabled as a result of polio. She met a young man who, despite the fact that she was very reserved as a result of her disability, became friendly with her, and then more than just a friend. At one point in the book, she overhears her parents, who are both doctors (father a psychiatrist, mother a paediatrician) discussing her young man. Her father says that the man is probably someone with a disability fetish, and that such men rarely make good husbands. Naturally the girl is upset, and determined that her young man will prove them wrong. As it turns out, the young man does not have a fetish or a specific attraction to disabled women, but it seems he is using the girl, who works for a firm of very high-class auctioneers, as he is actually part of a gang of thieves and he wants her to be the insider in helping the gang to rob the auction house. Because she is, by that stage, in love with him, she very reluctantly agrees, but after the robbery she discovers that what he has told her about himself is a tissue of lies. She has a change of heart and writes to the police, telling them what happened.

As a consequence of this novel, Lucy's view of men who wanted to get to know her because of, rather than in spite of her disability was once again somewhat coloured. However, another novel that she read gave her a slightly different perspective. (It was the case that, certainly at that time, novels featuring disabled people in prominent and sympathetic roles were extremely rare.) This novel was Arthur Hailey's *The Final Diagnosis.* One of the key characters in this was a young student nurse who starts dating a junior doctor. The relationship progresses to the point they become engaged. Then she gets a pain in her knee. Bone cancer is diagnosed, and she has her leg amputated. In this case, the young doctor realises he is put off (not attracted) by her disability, she senses his reaction, and she breaks off with him.

So these novels gave Lucy two scenarios – those men who are attracted to disabled women, and those who are put off by them. Both novels painted a rather bleak picture, which tended to reinforce her reluctance to get into a relationship. She thought back over her relationships and friendships. She knew that Zak had been neither attracted to nor put off by her amputation, having commenced the relationship before her accident. For him, it was an aspect of Lucy that just inadvertently came about, and she felt that he simply respected how she got on with her life regardless. Brian was a different matter. She knew he had been in love with her, and she had almost been on the point of falling in love with him – and would probably have done so if she hadn't still been getting over Zak's death. But when she had asked him about men who were attracted to her because of her amputation, his immediate embarrassment caused her to feel that he was 'turned on' by her one-leggedness. But he never mentioned it and he didn't make an issue of it, and was a nice person irrespective of what inner fantasies he might or might not have. At the time she had been the one with the prejudice against any such attraction.

Lizzie was very astute, and something of an amateur psychologist, and Lucy discussed with her this phenomenon of men who were attracted by her disability. Her take on it, reflecting what Morag had said, was practical, down-to-earth, and very wise.

"People come in all different types, and have all sorts of different likes and dislikes. Some men like girls with big boobs, or blue eyes, or red hair, or glasses." She gestured pointedly at Lucy's. "So why shouldn't they like girls who are deaf or blind or have only one leg? As long as they like the girl for who she is as a person, and not just her body. And some men can be creeps, regardless of what they like or dislike, while others can be gentlemen to their fingertips. If you reject every man who finds you attractive, Lucy, you'll have a very lonely life. But at the same time, be careful, and don't go near the creeps!"

The *be careful* reminded Lucy of what Helen had said regarding her relationship with Zak, not that he was a creep.

Lucy also found that some people, of both sexes, tended to regard her as something of a hero. She got comments about how inspirational she was, and how brave it was for her to be a university student with her disability. Lucy certainly didn't feel like a hero. She felt there was nothing heroic about it. She was simply living her life and making the best she could of the circumstances in which she found herself – indeed, what else could she do if she wasn't to simply wallow in a pit of self-pity and despair? Her accident certainly wasn't of her choosing, and there was nothing brave about it; it was simply a matter, having survived the accident, of necessity in adapting to the consequences. So these people she found rather annoying, and sometimes she let them know that she didn't appreciate their hero worship. While it was definitely preferable to the 'creeps', Lucy had no desire to be a role model, a hero, or some sort of saint that people looked up to. If she wanted adulation she preferred to get it from performing well in a concert.

After her second year at university, Lucy went back to Sussex as usual for the summer holiday period. She decided to get her hair, which she had always allowed to grow to its natural length, cut into a longish bob. While in some ways she missed her glorious long curly locks, she did find it easier to manage, and cooler in warm weather.

That summer (1976) was a long and unusually hot summer, so she and her mother drove down to Cornwall for two weeks (in Lucy's car, as Helen could also drive it, but Lucy couldn't drive Helen's, which was manual transmission). They stayed in bed-and-breakfast guest houses, swam in the sea, visited Roseland, St Michael's Mount, Lizard Point and Land's End, ate cream teas, and thoroughly enjoyed themselves.

Helen had heard from Susan that Brian had returned, after working in Australia for eighteen months, and was now a GP in Hampshire. Lucy noted the information with no sign of emotion, but inwardly she did wonder what would happen if she saw Brian again. She both hoped for and dreaded the possibility. She hoped for it because her views on Brian's attraction to her amputation had been modified and were now different; she really had liked him, she was well over Zak, and because she felt badly about the way she had left him and wanted to apologise. She dreaded the possibility because she didn't know how Brian would react – she had left him without even seeing him, and he might never forgive her, or he might have found someone else, or…

The only way, of course, for this to be resolved, was for Lucy and Brian to meet, but she was not going to take the initiative. Although Helen did not know what had happened between Lucy and Brian, and she had told her mother nothing of her reason for the suddenness of her departure from Australia, Helen was no fool and suspected that it was something to do with Brian. She saw no reason why a long-standing friendship between her daughter and her brother-in-law's nephew should not continue, so after she and Lucy returned from Cornwall, unbeknown to Lucy, she got Brian's contact details from Susan, telephoned, and invited him to come and visit them. He agreed, somewhat diffidently, to come on a Saturday in early August.

Helen specifically asked Lucy to stay at home that day, and said she wanted to do some baking and so would be busy in the kitchen if anybody called. Lucy was rather mystified by this, but accepted it at face value. Such was the state of play when, in the middle of the morning, the doorbell rang, Lucy answered it, and was faced with Brian standing there, with a large bouquet of roses, and an uncertain smile on his face.

CHAPTER EIGHTEEN

Courtship

✠

Lucy's jaw nearly hit the floor when she saw Brian standing on the doorstep. After a moment, she gathered her wits, took a step backwards on her crutches, and muttered, "Brian... I, uh, really wasn't expecting... You'd better, uh, come in... I never imagined..."

Brian's smile widened.

"It's okay, Lucy. Your mother invited me. Don't worry, I won't bite. I see you've had your hair cut. I loved your long hair, but you look equally beautiful with it shorter. Here, these are for you..." He handed her the roses. Lucy took them in her right hand, and half-hopped, half-crutched on her left crutch into the living room, followed by Brian.

"Sorry, I should have carried them in."

"No, it's okay. Sit down." Then, putting the roses on a table, she called loudly, "Mum! Brian's here!"

Helen's voice replied from the kitchen: "Okay. I'm busy in the kitchen. Brian, if you and Lucy want a coffee, come and get it."

Having just sat down, Brian stood up again, laughing. "I think we've been set up. Coffee?"

"Yes, I think we have. Okay, coffee."

Brian left the room. Lucy heard a murmur of voices in the kitchen, then after a minute or two he returned with two mugs of coffee and a plate with very fresh, home-baked shortbread, hot out of the oven, which he placed on the table beside the roses.

"Brian, I didn't arrange this. I'm really, really sorry I left you so suddenly in Sydney, without even saying goodbye. Please forgive me."

"Lucy, there's nothing to forgive. You had made it clear that you weren't sure you could be in love with me, you needed to think about it, so... you thought about it, decided, and left."

"Yes, but the reason I left was not because I couldn't have fallen in love with you – I probably could, but the timing was off – I was still getting over Zak." Here she hesitated, then took the plunge and explained. "I sensed that you had what I thought was an ulterior motive for wanting to be with me. I thought that you were attracted to me because of my amputation, and at the time I thought that was a bizarre and horrible reason to want to be with me."

Brian blushed. "Ah, you thought I was a pervert."

Now Lucy blushed. "Well... no... oh... maybe, I don't know. But anyway, I thought it a bit off. But I've come to realise that, as long as someone likes me as a person, if they like this too," she gestured at the empty space below her left hip, "then that's okay. I know there are some weirdos out there, but I also know you're not one of them."

"Lucy, you are the only person in the world, so far as I know, who has ever suspected that I am attracted to you for that reason. So yes, maybe I am a pervert, and maybe you were absolutely right to put more than ten thousand miles between us...

"But you are also right in that I do like you... No, that's the wrong word... I do *love* you for more than just that. Don't forget, I knew you – and liked you – long before your accident. And while I would never in a million years have wished the outcome of your accident upon you, when it happened it only made you even dearer to me. But when you did have your accident you were in a relationship with Zak, so I accepted my fate – that you and I were probably never destined for each other – and I went back to throwing myself into my studies and my medical practice.

"Then, when you turned up in Bangalore, for a moment it was like a dream come true, but then I saw how ill you were, and I was really worried. Thankfully, with the skill of Mr da Souza, you pulled through, and once again my hopes soared. But I didn't say anything because I knew you were still recovering – from the infection and the surgery, and also from what had happened with Zak. Then in Australia Ellen told you I was in love with you, and told me she had told you, and you made it clear it was not the right time.

"I suspected, when you left in such a hurry, that you might have discovered that I was attracted to you because of your particular, er, physical attributes. It didn't make it easier for me – I was pretty upset, and I've never even looked for anyone else."

"Oh, Brian!" Lucy stood up and hopped over to him, arms wide. He folded her into his arms, and held her. They both had tears in their eyes. "Brian, you are the sweetest man, and I think I really am falling in love with you," Lucy whispered to him.

They kissed, and clung to each other. Then Brian laughed.

"We'd better get those roses in some water."

The rest of the day passed almost in a dream for both of them. They had lunch with Helen, then went for a walk along the beach. Lucy had put on her leg (wearing one of the few pairs of relatively loose jeans she had that fitted comfortably over the socket, and which she hadn't cut to fit her stump) as she wanted to walk hand-in-hand with Brian, which wasn't possible on crutches.

Brian told Lucy that he was renting a flat close to his GP practice in Hampshire, but that he was thinking of buying a house – all the more so if there was a prospect of Lucy joining him at some point. Lucy told Brian she had one more year at university to complete to get her Dip.Ed. and Mus.B. degrees. A thought struck her.

"Brian, do you have to get back to your flat tonight?"

"Well, I had intended to, but I don't have to. I'm not on call tomorrow, though I have to be back for work on Monday. Why?"

"Could we go somewhere? Together? Overnight?"

Brian was taken aback by the speed at which things were progressing, but he was more than happy to oblige. Back at the house Lucy took off her leg and put on a swishy pleated skirt. She told Helen she and Brian were going out for the evening, and not to expect her back until the following day. Helen smiled knowingly.

They got into Brian's car and drove to a quiet country pub that served good food and also had rooms. Brian stopped briefly en route to buy himself a toothbrush and a razor (and a packet of condoms). Lucy had put her toothbrush into her bag.

Over a simple but excellent dinner, washed down with a bottle of wine, they talked.

"Brian, I am sorry I wasted so much of the time we could have been together by my hasty departure from Sydney."

"Lucy, darling, it doesn't matter, and it wasn't a waste of time. We both have a deeper understanding. Anyway, the past doesn't exist, there's only now."

Lucy laughed. "You sound like Swami Yogananda. Everything is illusion except the present moment."

"It's true. So let's not waste this moment by thinking of what might have been. If you go down the road of 'what might have been' you'll drive yourself crazy. Just think of it – what might have been if you hadn't had the accident, what might have been if you hadn't gone to India, what might have been if you had accepted Davy's suggestion to smuggle heroin, what might have been if the osteomyelitis in your residual leg hadn't been cut out... You really would go crazy thinking of all the possibilities, good and bad!"

"Yes, you're right. And Swami Yogananda was right. Brian Patterson, that was a wonderful meal, but that moment has now passed, and I want to enjoy the next one with the most gorgeous man that I've just realised I'm in love with."

"Oh! And who might that be?"

"Sweetheart, you know very well that it's you. Let's go upstairs."

So saying, Lucy stood up and slipped her arms into the cuffs of her crutches.

In the bedroom, Brian sat on the side of the bed.

"I haven't any pyjamas with me."

"I don't have a nightdress with me! Whatever shall we do?"

They both laughed.

Lucy sat next to Brian, laying her crutches on the floor. He put his arms around her, and they kissed – first lightly, lips brushing lips, then passionately, savouring each other...

That night Lucy discovered, to her astonishment and utter joy, just how her imperfect, one-legged body could become, to her lover, the most seductive and beautiful thing imaginable, and that he could be for her the gentlest yet strongest of beings, the perfect musician to play upon an instrument whose very imperfections made it even more beautiful.

Passion spent, they curled together, arms around each other, Lucy's leg between Brian's two legs, and drifted off to sleep. Waking in the morning was a gentle realisation of supreme happiness that they had finally accepted each other and were together. They made love again, slowly and more gently.

"You find me even more attractive and sexy because I have only one leg, don't you?" Lucy asked, putting on her glasses and stretching lazily.

"I never admitted it to anyone else, and I would never in a million years have wished it upon you, but yes, I do. But please, Lucy, sweetheart, let's just keep it between us. I could get struck off if it became known."

"Of course, darling. I'll never breathe a word to a soul. But I'm really, really happy that I have only one leg. I never imagined I could say that, and mean it, but I do. There were times I cried bitterly over losing my leg, but they are most definitely in the past. It certainly doesn't make life easier, but it's given me so much more. Not only am I the person I have now become because of it, but if I had two legs you wouldn't think I'm as beautiful as you do."

Brian smiled happily.

After breakfast they checked out, and went for a lazy drive, before returning to Helen's house in the afternoon, knowing that she would have gone to mass in the morning, it being Sunday. Later that evening, after an evening meal, Brian drove home having promised Lucy to spend the next weekend with her again.

There were, of course, several phone calls during the week. When Brian turned up the following Saturday morning, he went down on one knee in front of Lucy, produced a sapphire and diamond ring with a gold setting, and said, in time honoured fashion, "Lucy, darling, would you do me the honour of becoming my wife?"

Lucy squealed with delight, flung her arms around Brian, nearly beating him up with her crutches in the process, and said "Of course I will, darling."

Thus, they became engaged. Over the next six weeks, until Lucy returned to university, they spent as much time together as possible. They went house hunting in Hampshire, and found an attractive semi at a reasonable price, on which they made an offer, duly accepted. Brian had enough savings to put down the deposit, and they acquired a mortgage.

They agreed to wait to get married until Lucy graduated, so they made wedding plans for the following summer (1977). Lucy went back to university on cloud nine, and blissfully showed off her ring to Lizzie, who had equally good news, having also finally got engaged to her longtime sweetheart in Yorkshire.

Lucy's contact with Brian during the university terms was limited largely to telephone calls and the occasional quick weekend visit. At Christmas Susan came over from Ireland and she and Brian stayed with Helen and Lucy, then Lucy went to stay with Brian in their new house in Hampshire for New Year (Susan stayed on with Helen, returning to Ireland in early January 1977). At Easter Lucy again stayed with Brian, but the two of them did visit Helen.

The relationship between them continued to deepen, evolving beyond the initial jubilation of having overcome Lucy's views on 'amputee admirers' and Brian's feelings of guilt and shame at his own unbidden desires. Their bond, forged over many years and encompassing childhood friendship, trauma, escape from coercion, infection and illness, provision of safety and life-saving treatment, and the overcoming of their respective hang-ups, became a source of strength, a solid foundation upon which they were slowly building a new life. At the same time, the raw sexual attraction and lust of each for the other added the ultimate icing on their cake. They were blissfully happy.

Of course, as in any relationship, little storms occurred from time to time. Brian soon discovered that Lucy hated things left lying around on the floor. There was, of course, a practical reason for this – she found it awkward to bend down to pick them up – especially if she was on her crutches, but also when wearing her leg. Brian was contrite after the first time Lucy expressed annoyance over this, and tried to ensure that he didn't do this anymore.

For his part, Brian was mildly annoyed that Lucy tended to squeeze toothpaste tubes from the middle, instead of the end. Such is the nature of human relationships!

Lucy graduated in June 1977, and a month later she and Brian got married.

AFTERWORD

Many years have gone by since the events recounted in this story. Of those involved in it, a little must be outlined to bring things up to date.

Davy Wilson studied economics while in prison, and on release became a professional gambler. He moved to Las Vegas (on a visitor visa, the application for which made no mention of his drugs conviction), made millions and then lost it all again. Staying in America (as an illegal immigrant), he was last heard of living in a homeless shelter in New York.

Jessica Ellis, when released, didn't wait around for Davy. She worked for a time as a freelance artist, then set up a small second-hand bookshop. She co-habited with another former hippy who had also been to India, who died in 2005. In 2008 she sold her bookshop, and lives in quiet retirement.

Pete Clark, barred from practising as a doctor, became a paramedic some years after his release, working in the Ambulance Service. He retired in 2004. A gay man, he lived for a number of years with his partner, but in 1996 they parted. Pete now lives alone.

Kevin and Mandy returned from Australia. They were guests at Brian and Lucy's wedding. Subsequently they got married, but although they had children, they didn't stay together, and got divorced a few years later. Kevin, who remarried, worked for many years as a sound recordist for various media and television companies, retiring in 2007. Mandy qualified as a nursery nurse, and worked until she had children, a son and a daughter, and again after her divorce from Kevin, when her children went to school. She and Kevin, although divorced, are now grandparents.

Swami Yogananda continued to live in his ashram in Goa, with a circle of followers – mostly Indian but including a few westerners. According to his followers, in 2006 he entered a state of samadhi (where God consciousness is achieved and individual consciousness is merged into the universal) for the final time, and passed away in deep meditation. Lakshmi continued to be one of his followers to the end, and has since entered an ashram as a renunciate.

Cathy (Catriona) didn't have her leg amputated. Her post-polio syndrome was more advanced than either she or her parents realised. In her teens she started to experience weakness in her better leg, and before she was twenty she became a full-time wheelchair user. She married a farmer in the West of Ireland, had two miscarriages, and was never able to have children. Like many of her generation, she smoked and drank, and with already weakened lungs (which she also hadn't known about in childhood) she developed severe asthma, had pneumonia twice, and died in the early 1990s from chronic lung disease, only in her mid-forties.

Morag and Martin were guests at Brian and Lucy's wedding. Their own wedding took place shortly afterwards (Lucy and Brian attended). They live in Scotland and have four children and five grandchildren. Every Christmas, Morag and Lucy exchange Christmas cards.

Lizzie and her fiancé David were also guests at Brian and Lucy's wedding, and some months later they reciprocated as guests at theirs. Lizzie became a librarian, her husband a solicitor; they have one son who is now married and has two children. Lizzie and David still live in Yorkshire. Both are now retired.

Gerald and Margaret Butler lived in their big house in Foxrock until he retired in the late 1980s. They then sold up and moved into a luxury flat in Dalkey, just southeast of Dun Laoghaire. Gerald died in 2007, Margaret in 2015.

Philip Butler continued to work as a solicitor in London until 2004. He is married with a son and two granddaughters. He and his wife have retired to a village in Hertfordshire.

Ruth and Ben Goldberg were also among the guests at Lucy and Brian's wedding. Lucy reintroduced Ruth to Kevin, and suggested that Ruth gave the master tapes of the recordings that *Tangerine Sunset* had made be given to him, to see if he could do anything with them. Some days later Kevin did collect the tapes from Ruth, but discovered that they had been stored in a box full of odds and ends including some loudspeakers containing strong magnets. The magnetic radiation had virtually destroyed the recordings, so effectively *Tangerine Sunset* faded into darkness and obscurity. Ruth and Ben continued living in their big house for a number of years. Ben got Alzheimer's disease and gradually lost his memory, finally not even recognising Ruth. In the end he had to go into a nursing home, where he died in 1994. Ruth then sold the house and went to live with her daughter, Rebecca, and her family, in Manchester and died in 2007.

Patrick and Ellen flew over from Australia for Brian and Lucy's wedding. Patrick and Helen pointedly shook hands with each other, and Patrick introduced Ellen to Helen, joking that he had a wife and a partner whose names rhymed with each other. After staying in England for a couple of weeks they went to Ireland to visit Patrick's brothers and their families and his mother, Lucy's 'Granny Ryan', who was by then in her late eighties and living in a care home in Dublin, where she died in 1979. Returning to Sydney, Patrick eventually rose to be a sub-editor of his paper. He retired in 1989, and died as a result of a heart attack in 2008. Ellen had left her job with the network and became a freelance producer. She retired in 2002, looked after Patrick in his later years, and after he died she sold the house and moved into a flat in Sydney. She died in the Covid pandemic in 2021.

Brian's mother, Susan Patterson, continued living in her Georgian house in County Cork, a family inheritance, for many years, frequently travelling over to England to stay with Brian and Lucy, and with Helen. In the early 2000s she moved into a flat in a retirement village, and died peacefully in 2017.

Helen Ryan, Lucy's mother, now in her mid-nineties, continues to live in the house she and Patrick started renting when they first moved to Sussex in 1958, where Lucy spent most of her childhood, and where Barney is buried in the back garden. The rose bush still grows over his grave. Helen often stays with Brian and Lucy, and when her sister Margaret and Brian's mother, Susan Patterson, were alive used sometimes to travel over to Ireland to visit them.

Lucy and Brian still live in Hampshire, in a slightly bigger detached house that they bought in the early 1980s, with their dog, Rusty, and two cats, Tiggy and Fluff – the latest in a line of dogs and cats they have had since the early days of their marriage. After their wedding they honeymooned in the West of Ireland. They have since travelled to many places – including a safari in Kenya, a cruise around the Mediterranean, and another visit to Patrick and Ellen in Australia. They did consider going to Goa, but decided in the end that it was best to leave Lucy's memories of the place undisturbed.

They are both now retired. Brian worked as a GP until 2013. Lucy worked for a few years as a primary school music teacher, with breaks to have her own children. She also gave private violin and piano lessons, eventually doing this exclusively instead of teaching in school. For several years she also continued to play in a semi-professional string quartet. She and Brian are both members of a local community choir – Lucy as a soprano and Brian as a baritone, and Lucy – as a retired professional musician – is their deputy choirmaster and deputy piano accompanist (though she refuses to play the organ; she maintains that, with only one leg, she could not adequately play the pedals). They are also regular concertgoers.

Although no marriage is perfect, Lucy and Brian have had as near perfect a marriage as one can get. They are still very much in love with each other, and still find each other sexy. Lucy's amputation, to her surprise and delighted astonishment, has always been a boon to their marriage. She quickly discovered that one of her greatest physical pleasures in life (apart from actually having sex) was having Brian massage what she still calls her stump (that is her legless left hip area), and of course for him this was always a highly seductive activity, which almost invariably led to further erotic pleasures for both of them (and continues to do so now, even at their advanced ages).

Lucy and Brian had a daughter, Suzanne, and a son, Dermott, who are both now married and have children of their own. Despite her disability, Lucy found pregnancy relatively easy, though in both pregnancies from mid-term on she had to stop wearing her prosthesis, and in the last two or three weeks she found it easier to use a wheelchair. Other than this for many years she continued to eschew using a wheelchair, except at airports when travelling, when she admitted that airport assistance could be very convenient.

From the early 1990s she gave up wearing her prosthesis altogether for some twenty years, preferring the greater comfort and mobility afforded by her crutches. However in the early 2010s, with the advent of computerised knees (the 'C leg') and 'bikini' sockets, she has given wearing a prosthesis another go, and finds that, despite the physical effort involved, she can walk with a better gait on her new prosthesis than she ever could with her old one (better even than with the prosthesis she had when she was a transfemoral amputee), although since 2020 she has been using a walking stick as well. Conversely, she has also in recent years accepted the need to have a wheelchair (despite her reluctance), given her age and the increasing aches in her back, and remaining knee and hip. She uses it on outings that would otherwise involve too much walking to be comfortable. Around the house she still uses crutches. At Brian's insistence Lucy, from her mid-forties, gave up hopping around in the house for fear of damaging her good hip. She took to doing a one-foot shuffle if she needed to move a few feet and didn't want to bother with crutches.

For his part, Brian has also taken to using a walking stick. He thought of getting a rollator, but then realised that, when Lucy is in her wheelchair, holding the handles of this is just as good as any rollator.

With the advent of personal computers, and the internet, Brian was astonished to discover that there are lots of men around the world who share his aesthetic tastes when it comes to amputee women. There are many websites for 'devotees' (as admirers of amputee women are termed), and many pages of pictures and videos of such women. Some are obviously fake, but many are real. Some are posted by willing participants, which is fine, but others are pictures shot without the knowledge or consent of the woman. Brian regards this latter is a violation of these women's privacy. Although he spends little time browsing such sites, he has never found any unauthorised photographs of his beloved Lucy on the web. He is thankful that, by the time both the internet and mass photography using digital cameras – and especially mobile phone cameras – became so prevalent, Lucy was already at an age where she was less likely to attract unwanted and surreptitious 'peeping tom' photographers.

For her part, while Lucy is aware of the darker aspects of the internet, she balances this against the much higher profile that disabled people now have in modern life. After many years of the operation of anti-discrimination legislation, and the increasing coverage of the Paralympic Games and other disabled sports, she is optimistic that those with disabilities may have less to overcome than perhaps she did, although allowing that there is always room for improvement. Lucy has never for a moment felt that she was any less of a person because part of her body was missing, and has always maintained that discrimination against the disabled is frankly ridiculous because this is the one minority group that anybody at any time may inadvertently join, through disease, accident, natural catastrophe, or violence. Of course, to Lucy, any form of discrimination is anathema, having faced it as a child because of her Irish roots.

Lucy and Brian's son, Dermott, has become an accountant and has gone to live in Ireland with his wife Val and their two children. With Susan's blessing, they took over her Georgian house in County Cork when she moved out, maintaining the family connection with the property for further generations.

Suzanne, Lucy and Brian's daughter, with her husband Alan and their daughter Emily, live close to her parents. Brian and Lucy are doting grandparents.

When Ellen died in 2021, Lucy inherited the residue of her father's estate (which had been left for Ellen's use during her lifetime, but then to Lucy). This amounted to approximately three hundred and fifty thousand pounds. As she and Brian are comfortably off, she has been able to help her son and daughter financially, to set up trust funds for her grandchildren to see them through university if required, and to pay for a cleaner, a gardener and personal care assistant to help her mother.

Lucy still plays her violin (she still has both violins – the one her mother gave her, and the one Brian gave her), and sometimes the piano (she and Brian have a Broadwood baby grand piano in their living room).

She also still practices the meditation Swami Yogananda taught her so many years ago. She has found it a pillar of strength and stability in her life, as it was at the time of her dramatic departure from Goa after Zak's death. She has experienced several losses in her life – her leg, Zak, Barney and other subsequent much-loved dogs and cats, her grandmother, her father, her mother-in-law, and so on. She knows there will be future losses – her mother (given her advanced age), and, at some point, probably before she herself goes, her beloved Brian. While the pain of these has been and will be great, she accepts that, as Swami Yogananda said, the breath within her is the one thing she can hold onto until the moment both it, and she with it, leave her body.

From the moment Brian and Lucy realised they loved each other, Lucy has never regretted any aspect of her life, least of all her accident and amputation. Although she still has phantom sensations in her missing leg, which occasionally flare into phantom limb pain, Lucy maintains that she has learned so much from her amputation, primarily about herself, but also about the reactions of others, that she could never have known or understood otherwise; has gained so much inner strength; has revelled in overcoming the challenges it has posed her; and has come to regard her body as beautiful and sexy, just as it is. Brian would one hundred percent agree with her.

ACKNOWLEDGEMENTS

This story has been inspired by many sources, including, but not limited to: personal recollections, events, people and places that I knew or know (though no real person is depicted in this account).

Programmes and their signature tunes referred to as used on BBC radio in the 1960s are amongst those that I personally remember from that period.

Particular acknowledgement must be made to Richard Gregory's memoir of the Hippy Trail for background information, details of routes and descriptions of such places as The Pudding Shop in Istanbul, Freak Street and the Zigi Hotel in Kabul, etc.

The medical information and other practical aspects of life as an amputee are drawn from online sources, including the blogs and Instagram, YouTube or Facebook accounts of too many people to mention individually, as well as from personal accounts from people I know or have known. I must, however, give particular mention and thanks to the American author Kati Gardner (herself an amputee), whose novels *Finding Balance* and *Brave Enough* (although totally unrelated to this story) served as partial inspiration and provided some useful snippets of information. Throughout I have tried to be as accurate to the time-frame of the story (for example, in the types of prosthesis available in the early 1970s) as possible.

I am also indebted to William Barretto's online reminiscence *Travelling From Bombay To Goa By Steamer In The '60s & '70s*, which provided some of the background details included in my account of the journey by Lucy and her companions on that route.

Passing mention is made of many historical events which took place prior to or during the time-span of this story. These actually took place, and any inaccuracies are mine alone.

Finally, I would like to thank my editing and publishing team at KINDLE BOOK PUBLISHING for their invaluable help and assistance in bringing this book to fruition.

APPENDIX

The historical events the story refers to that took place prior to or during the time-span of this story:

The reign of Tipu Sultan in Southern India;

The establishment of the British "canton" in Bangalore, and the staffing of the garrison with Tamil soldiers from Madras;

The Irish War of Independence and Civil War;

The evacuation from Dunkirk in 1940;

The Ardennes campaign and Battle of the Bulge in 1944;

The Holocaust;

The Independence of India in 1947;

The ending of Portuguese colonisation of Goa;

The full independence of the Republic of Ireland in 1947;

The long hard winter of 1962/63;

The Cuban Missile Crisis of 1963;

The assassination of President John F Kennedy;

The death and funeral of Winston Churchill;

The IRA's destruction of Dublin's Nelson's Pillar in 1966;

The period of discrimination against 'Blacks and Irish' in England in the late 1950s and 1960s;

The Northern Ireland 'Troubles', which began in 1969;

The cultural revolution of the late 1960s and 1970s which spawned among other things 'flower power', mass usage by large numbers of young people of cannabis and psychedelic drugs, rejection of 'the establishment', the anti-war movement, and the hippy trail to India;

The Beatles 'falling-out' with Maharishi Mahesh Yogi;

The Vietnam War;

The conflict between Israel and Palestinians;

The long hot summer of 1976; and

The Covid pandemic of 2020/21.

ABOUT THE AUTHOR

Born in the mid-1950s, the author, Matthew R James, lives in semi-retirement in the UK with his wife and cat. This is his first novel.